HOLLY MARTIN lives in a little white cottage by the sea. She studied media at university which led to a very glitzy career as a hotel receptionist followed by an even more glamorous two years working in a bank. The moment that one of her colleagues received the much coveted carriage clock for fifteen years' service was the moment when she knew she had to escape. She quit her job and returned to university to train to be a teacher. Three years later, she emerged wide eyed and terrified that she now had responsibility for the development of thirty young minds. She taught for four years and then escaped the classroom to teach history workshops, dressing up as a Viking one day and an Egyptian High Priestess the next. But the long journeys around the UK and many hours sat on the M25 gave her a lot of time to plan out her stories and she now writes full time, doing what she loves.

Holly has been writing for 9 years. She was shortlisted for the New Talent Award at the Festival of Romance. Her short story won the Sunlounger competition and was published in the Sunlounger anthology. She won the Carina Valentine's competition at the Festival of Romance 2013 with her novel The Guestbook. She was shortlisted for Best Romantic Read, Best eBook and Innovation in Romantic Fiction at the Festival of Romance 2014. She is the bestselling author of 20 books.

Also by Holly Martin

A Home on Bramble Hill
One Hundred Proposals
One Hundred Christmas Proposals
Tied Up With Love

The Guestbook
at Willow Cottage

HOLLY MARTIN

ONE PLACE. MANY STORIES

HQ
An imprint of HarperCollins*Publishers* Ltd
1 London Bridge Street
London SE1 9GF

This paperback edition 2018

3
First published in Great Britain by
HQ, an imprint of HarperCollins*Publishers* Ltd 2018

Copyright © Holly Martin 2018

Holly Martin asserts the moral right to be
identified as the author of this work.
A catalogue record for this book is
available from the British Library.

ISBN: 9781848457713

MIX
Paper from
responsible sources
FSC
www.fsc.org
FSC™ C007454

This book is produced from independently certified FSC™ paper
to ensure responsible forest management.

For more information visit: www.harpercollins.co.uk/green

Typeset by Palimpsest Book Production Ltd, Falkirk, Stirlingshire
Printed and bound in Great Britain by
CPI Group (UK) Ltd, Croydon, CR0 4YY

Dear Guests,

Welcome to Willow Cottage, I hope you enjoy your stay. I'm only next door, so if there is anything at all that you need, please don't hesitate to let me know.

You may wish to use this guestbook to do a diary entry for every day you are here, tell us where you've been and what you've done. You may wish to leave helpful hints for other guests or you may just want to leave a short comment at the end of your stay telling me what you think of Willow Cottage.

I will come by on Tuesdays to drop off fresh towels, so if there's anything else you need, you can always write it in the guestbook and I will check on it then.

Annie Butterworth.

⚬

1st to 8th March
Rosie and Jake Hamilton

Saturday:
Thanks so much for the flowers and champagne, what a lovely surprise. The cottage is beautiful and Chalk Hill village is so cute. I'm so excited to be here. We're on our honeymoon – one long, delicious week with my beautiful hubby. Yesterday I married my best friend. I really am the luckiest girl alive.

Jake says we can go for long walks along the beach and explore the beauty of the Norfolk Broads. Personally, I

1

don't think we'll be leaving the house much. We've been here six hours already and we've only really seen the bedroom! We're getting a takeaway tonight, another excuse to stay in bed.

Can I just say for the record now, so it is here in black and white, I love my husband soooooo much. He won't read this so I'm safe.

Mrs Rosie Hamilton

(Mrs!! I don't think I'll ever tire of that!!)

Sunday:

I'm in love, did I mention that? I can't stop staring at the ring. It just hasn't sunk in yet. I'm married!! And to the most marvellous man as well. Jake caught me watching him sleep last night, bet he thinks he's married a right weirdo. Still, there's no escape for him now.

We actually made it to the beach today. The dunes are beautiful. We had a picnic and even had a dip in the sea.

Mrs Rosie Hamilton

What makes you think I won't read this? What you fail to realise is how much I love you too, even though you snore.

Jake Hamilton (Husband to Chief Snorer)

I do not snore.

You so do.

Monday:

Annie Butterworth, what a shock! With a name like Mrs Annie Butterworth, I was honestly expecting some grey-haired granny with half-moon glasses who would bring round homemade lemon drizzle cake. I didn't expect someone so young and pretty. Jake thought you were a ghost at first, seeing you run through the garden with your long white dress and blonde hair flying theatrically behind you. It was quite the entrance.

It was great talking to you today. Where is Mr Butterworth? You both must come round for dinner one night.

Love Rosie

As Rosie is using this as her own personal message board, it's down to me to say that today we hired a boat. Speedboat would be too much of a glamorous title for it. It was a row boat with an engine stuck to the back. Though even calling it an engine would be a stretch. It made a lot of noise and propelled us marginally faster than a snail. I haven't laughed so much in ages.

We ended up on some big lake and fed the swans our leftover picnic. The boat then failed to start and we were quite literally up s**t creek without a paddle.

Thankfully, some lovely Germans came to our rescue and towed us back to where we'd left the car. They didn't speak a word of English, or at least were not willing to. Though I didn't need to be fluent in German to know they were taking the piss out of us all the way back.

Jake

Tuesday:
Hi, Rosie, it was lovely to meet you too. I'm more than happy to come round with homemade lemon drizzle cake if that's what you were expecting. I don't have half-moon glasses, but I can wear my reading glasses if that will work. As for the ghost, I was always cast as the angel in the school plays, being a ghost would have been much more exciting.

Mr Butterworth – ha! Nick would have hated being called that – died two years ago, so he won't be joining us for dinner.

3

If the weather stays fine, how about you two join me for a barbeque tomorrow night?

Let me know if you want some eggs, Suzie and Doris, the chickens, are laying them faster than I can collect them.

Annie

Annie, I'm so sorry, I really need to engage my brain before I speak. I'm such a nosy cow. I just assumed that, as you were Mrs Butterworth, he was still around. I'm sorry.

Rosie, I just saw Jake, he said you wanted some eggs so I'm just popping them in the fridge. Please don't worry. I'm not in the least bit upset or offended by you asking where he is. It's been two years and though I miss him terribly, I really don't mind talking about him.

Annie, a barbeque will be lovely. We are taking a boat out to Blakeney Point to see the seals tomorrow and then going for a drive down the coast. I imagine we'll be back around seven. I'll bring burgers and chicken, that's if Suzie and Doris won't mind.

Jake

Wednesday:
We went out to see the seals today. It was amazing; we got so close to them. Jake took some fantastic pictures, he's always good with a camera. Many of them were swimming around the boat as curious about us as we were about them. Off to a barbeque round Annie's now, hopefully I won't put my foot in my mouth again.

Watching Rosie get so excited about the seals today, I think I fell in love with her a little bit more.

4

Thursday:
My head hurts.

Annie is quite possibly one of the loveliest people I have ever met in my entire life. I didn't stop laughing all night. She looks so sweet and innocent in her pretty flowery dress and huge Jesus sandals. She looks like she goes to church every Sunday and probably sings in the choir, so it comes as a bit of a shock when the stories she comes out with are so funny and sometimes even filthy.

We must have polished off at least two bottles of wine and too many bottles of cider to count between us. That cider was potent, some obscure local variety I think. By the end of the night Jake was a mess and I was even messier. Annie, however, looked as fresh as a daisy.

Did I put my foot in it? Yes, probably about a hundred times. I felt like John Cleese in *Fawlty Towers* when the Germans came: 'Whatever you do, don't mention the war.' I just couldn't stop mentioning her husband, death or funerals. Luckily Annie saw the funny side.

I was not a mess, at least I didn't throw up in my shoe this morning. Great night, Annie, thanks for the amazing cider, we need to get hold of a few bottles before we leave.
    Jake

Just popped in to change the lightbulb in the bathroom. I'm definitely getting a change of wardrobe after that lacklustre description ;-) I don't go to church apart from weddings, christenings and funerals. Oh no, I mentioned the funeral word!!! I can assure you I wasn't feeling as fresh as a daisy this morning, my tongue felt drier than Gandhi's flip-flop. I'll get you some of the cider to take back with you.

Friday:

After recovering from our excessive hangover yesterday, we spent the day in the garden reading. Jake wears his big glasses when he reads, he thinks it makes him look clever, but he looks more like a nerd. A loveable nerd though. He was reading some big tome on codes used in WWII. Geek! Another day on the beach today. Wells-Next-The-Sea really is the loveliest place in the world, the beaches are spectacular.

Geek? Nerd? How dare you? Besides, I don't think I look clever, I know I'm clever. Never mind the fact that I fell asleep four times reading the code book. It was the hangover that was having an adverse effect on me. Anyway, what were you reading, the third book in the *Fifty Shades of Grey* trilogy, wasn't it? Pervert.

I'll have you know, the *Fifty Shades* trilogy has a very good storyline. And, yes, you are a complete geek and a nerd, but I still love you.

Saturday:

Annie, we have had the best time. We are going to come again soon. We don't live that far away so we're going to drive down when you have some free weekends.

Yes, I came here for a quiet week away after all the stress of the wedding, but we're definitely going to be coming back on a regular basis. Willow Cottage is beautiful. Thanks so much for making us so welcome.

❧

8th to 14th March
Oliver ~~Butterworth~~. Black

Saturday:
I'm here to kill someone and I'm not leaving until I've done it.

Sunday:
I'm thinking of using a scythe, with a jagged, serrated edge. Though I don't want my victim to die too quickly; it needs to be slow and painful, it needs to be bloody. I want her to see her blood drain out of her, slowly, agonizingly feel her life force ebb away. I want her to beg for her salvation. I want that tough, hard exterior to crumble in the last pitiful minutes of her pathetic life. I want to see her cry.

My best-laid plans continue to go awry. As devious as I am in trying to catch my prey, she is as cunning at evading me. I almost respect her for it. Almost.

Oh, Olly, you do make me laugh. It's good to have you back. You do realise how this will look, don't you, or is that your intention? I'll have the police on me for harbouring a criminal. If they come for me, I'm taking you down with me. There's no honour amongst thieves.
 Annie x

Careful, Annie, or I may have to kill you.

Oh please do, I've been begging you to kill me off for years. The bloodier and messier, the better. Could you chop off my head and tear out my innards? Could you gouge out my eyes and keep them about your person as a memento? You could have a whole box of eyes left over from your victims. Oh, and could

7

you write some message on the walls using my blood? My brain could be the full stop. I'd love that.

I bet you would, you sicko. Now, leave me alone. I came here for some peace and solitude, not to be bothered every five minutes by the dodgy landlady next door. If you disturb me again, I really will consider ripping out your heart and letting you watch as it beats feebly in my bloody hands.

Promises, promises. Come for dinner tonight, don't shut yourself away for the whole week. I've missed you. If you come, I promise to be good and quiet for at least a day.

Right, that's it, you're in for it now. I need a big knife.

I have one. You're welcome to come round and borrow it.

Monday:
After dinner with my sister-in-law, I feel much better about the murder. We talked things through and she gave me some great ideas on how to commit the perfect crime. I now know how I'm going to dispose of the body too. No one will ever find her. Claudette Montana is going to die tonight. I will not rest until she is lying in the ground.

Claudette Montana? Really? Please kill me off, not her.

I am not killing you off. I've told you before, Annie Butterworth just isn't sexy enough to be in one of my books. Annie Butterworth sounds like an old granny with fluffy slippers and someone who wears cardigans, no matter how hot it is. Why do you think I changed my name to Oliver Black? Oliver Butterworth would be smoking a pipe and sucking on his

8

Werther's Originals, he certainly wouldn't be the number-one crime writer in Britain, nay, the world.

You think a lot of yourself, don't you? And yes, I'm well aware I'm not sexy enough for you.

Are we still talking about the book here? Let's not go down that weird road again. Besides, you were in my last book, you obviously didn't look hard enough.

I was not, I would have noticed that.

Try the very front of the book.

What's this? The Great Oliver Black having writer's block? Surely not.
   Sophia Lorenzo. Cleaner.

Oh, Annie. Please tell me, with all your money, why you still haven't got yourself a decent cleaner yet? Why do you still have that old bag hanging around like a bad smell?

Oliver Butterworth, don't think you are too old to be put over my knee.

Oh, Auntie Sophia, are you still mad that I killed you off in Behind Closed Doors?

I was more bothered that you made me into a prostitute.

High-class escort, actually, I couldn't resist. Besides, Sophia Lorenzo is a much sexier-sounding name than Annie Butterworth.

You dedicated your last book to me!! How did I miss that? I can't believe you did that. That's... thank you.

Oh, don't get all soppy on me. Jeez, if I knew it was going to get this reaction I would have dedicated it to my local Chinese takeaway, who kept me fed through the duration of the book.

And, Sophia, it wasn't so much writer's block, more murderer's block. I had made the character of Claudette so clever, under-handed and cunning that she wouldn't fall for the plots and ploys of Maxwell Hunt. I also needed to make sure the reader would feel sympathetic towards him; they had to want Claudette dead almost as much as he did.

Tuesday:
It is technically Tuesday. 3:27 a.m. on Tuesday morning to be precise. But Claudette has been killed. I feel like singing 'Ding dong! The Witch is Dead'. I have cracked open a bottle of Whin Hill Cider to celebrate, but may sneak next door and top up my celebrations with some of Annie's amazing trifle.

Note to self: when breaking into your sister-in-law's place, either go blindfolded or call out to make sure she is decent first. I don't know who was more shocked when I walked in to find her stark-naked, tucking into the trifle. Admittedly we're experiencing one of the hottest springs since before dino-saurs roamed the earth but, still, one should wear a robe when wandering about downstairs.

Why should I wear a robe in my own house? Normally my guests don't just take it upon themselves to wander into my house and help themselves to my food. That's not part of the service. Besides, you have seen me naked before.

10

Yes. You've put on weight since the last time.

Oh my god! Thanks very much!

Annie! You know very well that I meant that as a good thing. You were a bag of bones the last time I saw you. I'm so glad you're eating properly again now.

Nag, nag, nag.

I'm just saying, what I saw in the light of the fridge for those brief seconds was damned sexy.

Sexy enough to be in one of your books?

No.

If you won't kill me off, how about making me into a murderer instead?

Annie Butterworth, blonde hair, blue eyes, face like an angel, cast as an evil murderer, who would believe it?

Wednesday:
My sister-in-law has gone mad. Maybe the grief of my brother dying has finally got to her and it's pushed her over the edge. She tried to kill me three times yesterday.

The first time she leapt out of a cupboard with an axe. Scared the bloody crap out of me, but only because she was screaming like a banshee. When I turned around and saw Annie brandishing an axe in her little flowered blouse and denim shorts with those stupid oversized sandals she loves so much, I burst out laughing. It was hardly the scariest thing I've ever seen.

The second time, a quiche appeared in my kitchen with a

packet of rat poison next to it. The quiche tasted amazing, Annie always could cook.

I had to give her points for trying on the third attempt. I woke to find her straddling me, dressed head to toe in a black leather catsuit, her hair slicked back, her eyes lined with black and a knife pressed to my throat. I must admit, she did look mean, but I was too busy trying not to be turned on to be scared of her. Quite frankly, if she had killed me then I would have gone with a huge grin on my face.

Annie, you just don't have it in you to be a killer. I've seen you stop the car for a frog to cross the road. You didn't even have the guts to use a real knife, you had a spoon handle pressed to my throat.

I didn't want to hurt you. I could be believable as a killer, just you wait and see.

Thursday:
Annie may be a better killer than I thought. Last night I nearly died laughing.

She had made a dummy by stuffing old clothes with newspapers, a head out of an old melon and fastened it all together to look like a body, then wrapped it in a black binbag. Just as it was starting to turn dark, she went out to her front garden and, in full view of the rest of the village, dug a hole to bury the body. She obviously wanted to raise suspicions and prove that people would think she was capable of such a thing.

She was in luck. David Lambeth, the local constabulary, was driving past and he stopped when he saw her digging. I think she nearly did a little victory dance that he was going to ask her what she was doing, and make her explain the body-shaped bag on her front lawn. But instead, without a word, David went to the shed, grabbed another spade and helped her to dig the hole, only stopping once to clarify how deep she wanted it. I laughed so much I think I ruptured something inside.

Even when I told him I wanted the hole six-feet deep, he didn't bat an eyelid. I did relent in the end and told him I'd finish the hole the next day. He's coming round later to help me finish it off.

Friday:
I'm being kicked out today. Apparently a paying guest is more important than family.

You can stay in my spare room, you know that. I promise not to jump you.

I'd prefer to keep the boundaries a bit stricter, after last time.

Prude.

I'll be back for the grand re-opening of The Painted Plate. Take care, Annie. Sophia, take care of her.

I will. Don't stay away so long next time. Sophia x

⚬

14th to 17th March
Mrs Applecroft

Friday:
The last time I was here, Mrs Butterworth was grieving the death of her husband. The place was a mess.

I appreciate that the upkeep of Willow Cottage was not high on her list of priorities when she was trying to organise a funeral but, still, I would have expected some standards. When my husband passed away, I made sure the house was cleaned every day.

However, Wells-Next-The-Sea is a beautiful place and as I had been a regular guest up until the week of the funeral, I thought I would come back and give Willow Cottage one more chance.

I'm pleased to see the place has been redecorated and, although some of the décor is not to my taste, the house is mostly clean.

Mrs Applecroft

My apologies that Willow Cottage was not up to the usual standards you had come to expect the last time you were here. It's such a shame that you have stayed away because of that. We have missed you and your _very_ helpful advice on how to improve the cottage. I know Sophia, especially, will be delighted you are back.

I did let things slip a bit when Nick died, and I have never forgiven myself for not being clean and tidy in the months after his death. It is a burden I will have to live with for the rest of my life. Hopefully we can go some way to restoring your faith in us this time. After all, Cleanliness is next to Godliness.

Annie Butterworth

You are so right.

I have just been for a walk on the beach and though it is still beautiful, I was angered to see there were horse faeces on the path leading down to the sea front.

Disgusting! If dog owners have to pick up after their pets, horse owners should be no different.

Have watched four men leave Sophia Lorenzo's house in the last two hours. Her husband is seemingly away on business. While the cat's away...

The sign to Butterworth Farm is squeaky and in need of oiling.

Annie Butterworth singing in her back garden is disturbing my reading.

Saturday:
The sun shines too brightly through my bedroom window; it might be an idea to invest in some blackout curtains. The pillows are hard. The birds singing also disturbed me from my sleep.

I see young Shellie Gillespie stayed over with Michael Atkinson last night, I saw her leave his house very early this morning. It seems the tiny village of Chalk Hill has become a hotbed of sin.

Just got back from a walk round the shops. I was disappointed to see the wool shop has been replaced by some crass-looking cake shop.

Sunday:
Sophia Lorenzo disturbed my breakfast to come and clean. I must tell her about the dust on top of the wardrobes. I will leave a note. I don't feel comfortable reprimanding the help.

The help???

Firstly, if you'd had the decency to cancel your booking when we told you about Nick's death, you wouldn't have come at the worst possible time in Annie's life.

Secondly, the four men that left my house on Friday night were all builders and decorators who were giving me a quote for a new fitted bathroom. I may be bloody amazing in bed, but even I could not satisfy four men in less than two hours.

Thirdly, Shellie Gillespie is now married to Michael Atkinson and was leaving early to go to work but, even if they weren't married, this is the 21st century and what consenting adults do behind closed doors has nothing whatsoever to do with you.

Fourthly, if you want to climb up on top of the wardrobe and dust it, be my guest.

Sophia

After speaking to Mrs Lorenzo earlier today, I feel compelled to say how clean I have found the place. Furthermore, I will definitely be back. Willow Cottage is delightful. My sincere apologies if my previous comments did not do the cottage justice.

⚬

18th to 21st March
Hetty O'Donahue

Tuesday:
Hetty, I'm so looking forward to seeing you again. I know you won't mind, but I'll be popping in and out during your stay to see to the garden, it's got a bit tangled of late.

Annie x

My lovely Annie, the garden looks great but yes, of course, you can come in and tend to it. The house looks spectacular. I loved it before, but now it's amazing. I'm so glad to be back.

Hetty x

I'm so glad to have you back. The money to do up the place came from Nick. He was apparently insured up to the hilt. It seemed a fitting tribute to him to use the money to do up Willow Cottage, given that it started as an on-going project for us five years ago. I wanted to make it into the place we always dreamed it would be.

I have also used some of the money to renovate The Painted Plate, my little pottery painting studio. It has sat closed ever since his death, as I couldn't face working with the public anymore. It seemed weird that people would come in, happy, cheery, life continuing as normal when my life had stopped. I couldn't bear it. But I'm in a really good place now and the grand re-opening is in a few weeks. We're just doing Sundays and Tuesdays to start with. I really need to be around to greet guests when they arrive in the peak season on Saturdays. Chloe Sayles is going to be trained up as my Saturday girl so she can run the place for me on those days in the summer.

You're looking good. I'm so happy you are on the mend. Would Oliver have anything to do with your beautiful smile being back on your face?

Olly was a great help after Nick died. It's safe to say I wouldn't have got through those first few months without him. The whole of Nick's family were so supportive, especially Sophia and Olly. He stayed with me for nearly seven months, helping me get through each day one step at a time, he sorted out the insurance, bills, everything. We grew very close, but now we are just friends.

You three used to be as thick as thieves growing up. Mary Gillespie and I always used to joke that you had two boyfriends and would probably end up marrying them both.

I loved them both, still do. Though I think what I have with Olly is a brother/sister kind of love. Hell, you've seen him in the magazines, on the arm of a different woman every week, turns up to all those glamorous parties and premieres. He's hardly going to give up all of that for me.

Why does he have to give it up? He's a writer. He can write anywhere and, it seems, reading some of the other messages, he gets his best ideas around you. The parties and glitzy lifestyle are only a small part of his life. At the end of the day, he still wants a place to call home.

You're talking like this is an option. Sometimes he can hardly bear to look at me.

Well, after the accident he probably felt guilty, he was driving after all. He probably thinks he could have done something to prevent it.

It wasn't his fault, he knows that. I don't blame him.

Yes, but he's alive, Nick's not. He's bound to feel guilty about that, regardless of where the blame lies.

You should go and see Butterworth Farm whilst you're here, William would love to see you.

Nice change of subject there. OK, I won't say any more about it. For now. And are you *still* trying to get me and William together? Unless I had black and white spots and went moo, William wouldn't give me a second glance. He loves them cows.

He does, but he likes you too. There were five calves yesterday, there may be more today, little newborn babies, surely you can't resist.

I may pop over.

If you do, pop in and take some muffins and eggs with you. I also have some shepherd's pie I made for him; there'd be plenty left over for you tonight if you didn't want to cook.

I saw the cows, the little ones were very cute. William said ten words to me the whole time I was there.

Ten, really?

Yep, I counted them.

Oh dear.

Wednesday:
I found an engagement ring on the beach this morning, beautiful little thing, a diamond the shape of a teardrop and two clusters of tiny sapphires on either side. It looks antique. Makes me wonder how it got there. Was the girl lost at sea, did it belong to a sailor who lost his bride to scarlet fever and wore it as a memento of his sweetheart? I wonder how long ago it was given as a token of some man's affection.

Hetty, you old romantic, I hate to break it to you, but knowing Sally Jenkins down the road it probably belongs to her. She has been engaged more times than I've had hot dinners; to the same man three times and to eight others at the last count. She never marries them though. Lucky thing seems to have men practically queuing up to offer their hand in marriage, always some rich bachelor too. At book club last night, she told us the last one, Lord somebody or other, had the audacity to give her a cubic zirconia ring instead of a diamond one, apparently it ended up in the sea, along with the rings of the other men that either cheated or lied to her.

I'd be grateful to get any kind of ring. I'm still tainted at the moment, the grieving widow. Half the eligible bachelors in the village and surrounding areas, of which there aren't many, look at me like I'm an unexploded bomb and they're scared I may go off at any time. They let me win at pool in the pub and they never charge me for car repairs, just in case I might start crying again. The other half still see me as Nick's and think it would be disloyal to him to go behind his back and court me.

I'm not really looking for a man at the moment. It's still hard to think of being with another man that's not Nick. But although I'm not in the market, an appreciative glance wouldn't go amiss, instead of the looks of pity or fear I get from most men.

You need to get away. You're welcome to come and stay with me in Tenby. I can take you over to Skomer. If you come in a few weeks there'll be hundreds of puffins.

Olly said the same thing when he was here. He's offered me his beach house in California. I may go there for a few weeks before the peak season hits.

Tenby Beach or California? Lord, I know which I'd choose.

Though I do have the added bonus of my lovely gardener, Connor. He is the most beautiful man I have ever seen. The most amazing arms, so muscular, thick, strong thighs, lovely hands. I do so love a man who is good with his hands. If I was thirty years younger, I wouldn't mind having a go myself. He might be just what you need as a distraction.

Thursday:
Mmm, Tenby is looking more and more tempting. To see the puffins, of course.

Yes, maybe Connor could take you over to Skomer to see them. There are loads of secluded remote sections of the island.

Haha, Hetty, you are wicked.

Come for dinner tonight and we can discuss this in person rather than through the medium of this book.

Not my fault, you always seem to be out when I pop in.

Not to burst your bubble, my lovely, but I do have other people to see whilst I'm here. I'm cramming in as many morning teas, lunches and afternoon cake sessions as I possibly can with the lovely people of Wells. I'll squeeze you in at seven tonight.

I'm honoured.

Friday:
It's been lovely seeing you again, Annie. It was great chatting to you last night and I'm so looking forward to

paying back your hospitality in Tenby in a few weeks.
Give my love to William, that'll freak him out.

❧

21st to 24th March
Mr and Mrs Slater

Saturday:
Thank you for the welcome basket and flowers. We are looking forward to a nice quiet weekend away. George is especially looking forward to the fishing. Thank you so much for the book on fishing and the bucket of ragworms you left us. I never thought I'd be saying thank you for them. They are the most hideous, disgusting creatures I have ever laid eyes on, but George is delighted. I am reliably informed that ragworms are an excellent sea-fishing bait.
  Mrs Slater

The fishing is spectacular. I caught two big bass and a pollack today. We are barbequing the bass later.
  George Slater

Sunday:
The little beach huts are so cute. Is there any way to rent one for the day or weekend?

Just popped by to drop off some eggs.
  Most of the beach huts are owned by families and passed down through the generations. Many of the huts have been there since the Victorian era, though there are many newer ones. There are a few on sale for around 50-60k and a handful that are rented out in the summer months. I think if you just

type into Google 'beach huts, Wells-Next-The-Sea' you'll be able to find a few companies that rent them out.

Nick and I rented one for a week for our honeymoon. We slept there, even though we weren't supposed to, on sleeping bags and air mattresses on the floor, there was nothing more exciting than waking up and opening the door and stepping out onto the beach every morning. Pure heaven.

Annie

Annie, dear, I'm 73, George is 76, we don't have much need for Google.

I'll get you the telephone number. If you let me know what dates you are interested in, I'll email them on your behalf and find out if they have any availability and what kind of price you're looking at.

Monday:
We've had a wonderful stay and George is most impressed with the fishing. Thanks for the help with the beach hut. We may rent one in the summer, but we'll stay here too; we're too old to be sleeping on the floor at our time of life.

⚬

28th to 31st March
Mike and Sarah Littleton and bump.

Friday:
What a beautiful cottage. I love the log-burner. I definitely want to come back in the winter and sit by a big fire whilst the wind is roaring outside. Of course, we'll be a threesome

then. Our bump, getting bigger by the day, is due in four weeks. Mike is sure it will be a boy. I have a feeling it's a boy too, but I wind him up that's it's definitely a girl. He kicks a lot, so he'll probably be a footballer. Or an Irish dancer.

Sarah

Ha, I knew it was a boy! For the last nine months I've felt sure it was a boy. Just from the way you are carrying our bump and your cravings, the books say it's probably a boy too. That's it then, when we get back, I'm painting the nursery blue.

Annie, do you have a hot water bottle by any chance, Sarah's back is hurting. We're going down the beach now – if you read this before we get back and you have one, just leave it in the kitchen. By the way, the phone reception from the house is not great, any ideas where I can put a call through?

Thanks, Mike

I've left you a hot water bottle in the kitchen and a bottle of my favourite bubble bath, a good soak might help to ease the aches a bit. Go to the bottom of the garden to make calls, phone reception is good there.

Annie

The beach is lovely. Shame I had to cut our walk short, bloomin' Braxton Hicks. I've had them for the last two weeks now and they're getting closer and more painful. Perfectly normal, says my nineteen-year-old male doctor when I went to see him last week. He even told me they weren't that uncomfortable. How the heck would he know? I felt like kicking him in the balls and asking him whether that was uncomfortable. Thanks for the hot water bottle, Annie. I'm off for a bath and then an early night.

Sarah

Saturday:
Braxton Hicks continues. According to my prepubescent doctor, walking is good for it. So we're going down to the beach today. I'm determined not to spoil our last holiday together by sitting around the house moaning. The weather is beautiful, so I'm going to make the most of it.

Personally, I would prefer her to take it easy, but there's no persuading her to sit still.

Managed to persuade her to sit on the beach today rather than walking too far. She's so uncomfortable, bless her. Another early night, but she's not sleeping well either.

Shit, Shit, Shit!

SUNDAY:
AS VISITORS TO WILLOW COTTAGE, WE FELT COMPELLED TO WRITE IN THE GUESTBOOK. BABY LITTLETON WAS BORN THIS MORNING AT 2.27A.M. BABY WEIGHED IN AT 7LBS 2OZ. MOTHER AND BABY DOING WELL.
   JIM AND KATIE, PARAMEDICS

We would like to welcome into the world our new baby. Willow Rose took us quite by surprise a little after midnight. By the time the paramedics got here, the head was already out. She was delivered shortly after. She is quite possibly the most beautiful baby I have ever seen in my whole life. I know all mums say that, but she really is stunning. Mike was amazing, so calm and together. Though reading his previous comment, maybe he was panicking under the surface just like I was. Although mine was more on the surface panicking.
   Sarah

How can I fall in love with her so quickly, so immediately? I cannot stop staring at her. She is perfect in every way. We didn't have a girl's name; we were both so sure it was going to be a boy. But Willow, after the cottage, seems to fit perfectly. Sarah was fantastic, so brave.

  Mike

I can agree. Willow Rose is the most beautiful baby in the world. A first for Willow Cottage. We've not had babies stay here before, let alone be born here. What a wonderful surprise to wake up to this morning.

  Annie x

Just came round to check on the mother and baby. Both seem to be doing well. Willow Rose is a good weight and is feeding well.

  Sally Jenkins, Midwife

  PS Annie, the house looks amazing. x

Monday:

We're extending our stay by a few days. We need to get a car seat to take Willow home and Mike is not willing to leave us alone just yet to go and buy one. My parents are driving up from Cambridge and are going to stay in the other room. They are bringing all the things we need and we may go home Wednesday or Thursday. Luckily Annie doesn't have any other guests coming until the weekend.

OUR BABY GRANDDAUGHTER IS BEAUTIFUL AND WHAT A LOVELY PLACE FOR HER TO BE BORN. THANK YOU, ANNIE, FOR ACCOMMODATING US AT SUCH SHORT NOTICE.

  MR AND MRS BAXTER (SARAH'S PARENTS)

Tuesday:

Annie, thanks so much for the rubber ring. It is painful to sit down at the moment, how very thoughtful.

Thursday:
We're going home today. Thanks so much for having us. I can't believe how our life has changed so much over the last few days.

Love Sarah, Mike and Willow Littleton

5th to 19th April
The Meechams

Mrs Butterworth, the house is beautiful. Thank you so much for the Easter eggs for Megan and Isabelle, that's so thoughtful.

Mrs Meecham

My egg had chocolate buttons with bits on top and a puzzle on the back. Isabelle's had Smarties, so I had half of hers and she had half of mine. I found a shell that looked like a cat today. It even had ~~wisskers~~ whiskers.

Megan, age 6 ½

Tuesday:
I'm so glad you liked the eggs, Megan, and that you are enjoying the beach. If you would like to see some baby cows, let me know and I'll take you up to Butterworth Farm.

Annie Butterworth

Thursday:
The cows are so cute. Eight baby calves. William said I could name the baby ones. I called them Jake, Bella, Fizz, Milo, Dora, Daisy, Spot and Splat. Splat is called Splat because he did a big splat when I was stroking him. Splat is my favourite. Spot has a white spot on her face. Isabelle liked Spot best.

Megan

Friday:

There was a sandcastle building competition on the beach today. Me and Daddy and Isabelle made a huge one with turrits and flags and shells and we came second and won ice creams. I had chocolate with nuts and marshmallows and chocolate buttons.

Saturday:

We saw the seals today. We went on a boat and saw them. One was very fat and had big eyes.

Sunday:

It rained so we played on the Wii. I beat Daddy at the boat game, but Mommy was better than me.

Tuesday:

It's still raining but I have a puzzle book. Isabelle has a colouring book which I am helping her with. It also has stickers. My puzzle book doesn't have stickers.

You can come round and help me make cakes if you want; I need help with the icing part too.
  Annie x

Thursday:

Found a frog in the garden. I drew his picture and Mommy helped me to take his photo on her phone and put it on her Facebook. I called him Slimy.

Good Friday:

I met Mr Butterworth today. He was nice and funny. When I asked him if he was Annie's husband she said no but he said yes. But he must be if she is Mrs Butterworth and he is Mr Butterworth. He is here because there is a plate opening tomorrow. I'm not sure how a plate can open but Mommy says we can go along before we leave and I can paint something. Daddy says he loves Mr Butterworth. He kept shaking his hand and saying how much he loved him.

Good Saturday:
We all went to the plate opening today. I painted a frog just like Slimy. I gave him purple spots because I like purple. Isabelle had her hands and feet painted and put on a plate. She cried. Mr Butterworth also painted a mug that said he was the world's best writer. There was lots of glasses of wine but I had a glass of orange juice in a special wine glass.

Annie, we have had the best time and you have made the girls feel so welcome. Thank you so much.
Love Rebecca, Ben, Megan and Isabelle Meecham

✄

19th to 21st April
Oliver ~~Butterworth~~. Black

I'm glad I get to stay here tonight. The spare bed in Annie's house is very uncomfortable.

The grand re-opening of The Painted Plate was a huge success. The press turned up and there were even a good number of customers. Not bad for Annie's first day. So many of the locals turned up as well, to support her, which was lovely. They all love her here, that much is clear. I wasn't comfortable with the questions the press were asking about the reason The Painted Plate had stayed closed for so long. I just palmed them off with tales of decorating and renovating. Thankfully they were only local press and not the damned paparazzi that hounded us after Nick had died.

After flying in from New York yesterday, I'm feeling so jet-lagged it's like I'm drunk. My mind is racing and I'm clearly not thinking straight. I just offered to accompany Annie on a walk on the beach. She always goes for a stroll on the beach after dark, she's done it as far back as I can remember. Why I felt the sudden compulsion to go with her, I don't know. It's a recipe for disaster; moonlit stroll along the beach, the waves lapping gently on the sand, the deserted solitude, my beautiful best friend, what on earth am I thinking? What's worse is that I'm now putting my innermost feelings in this damned book.

~~I have already betrayed my brother in the worst possible way just six months after he died, I can't let it happen again. I just have to remember that she's my brother's wife, she is not the girl who rode on the back of my bike as a kid, she's not the girl I shared my first kiss with. She is my brother's wife, nothing more than that. Arghhh, why am I writing this stuff?~~

Sunday:
Early hours Sunday morning. I'm so tired now, think I've been awake for thirty-nine hours. Of course we sat on the beach and talked, of course she got cold and I put my arm round her, of course she sat next to me with her head on my shoulder. I didn't do anything. She's my brother's wife.

Oh, Olly!

Woken up around lunch with breakfast in bed. Annie is a wonderful cook and I'm feeling a lot better now that I've slept. Yesterday was just the inane ramblings of a madman.

Flying back out to New York tomorrow, for which I am thankful for.

I did not go for a walk with Annie tonight.

Monday:
Take care ~~my~~ Annie xx

❧

25th to 28th April
Rosie and Jake Hamilton

Friday:
Hi again Annie, just back for a weekend. It's so sweet that Willow Littleton was born here.
   Jake and I are in the middle of doing up our new home, so it's nice to have a break even if it is only for a few days.
   Rosie

Hi, Annie. It's good to be back.
   Jake

Saturday:
Another day at the beach today. I could walk on that beach every single day, I love it here. I'm trying to persuade Jake to move.

Whoa! The power has just gone out. We've not had any dinner yet.

A quick check has revealed that the whole village of Chalk Hill is out and, by the sounds of it, all of Wells-Next-The-Sea is out too.

Wow! What an amazing night. Shortly after the power went down and we were wondering what we were going to do for food, someone set up a barbeque on the village green. People started coming out of their houses with burgers, chicken, sausages and whatever else they had in their fridges. Annie told us to come out too, even though we didn't have anything to contribute towards a barbeque. There was so much food and drink that everyone in the village was catered for. Someone built a big fire and many people returned to their houses to bring out blankets and duvets. We all sat together well into the night eating each other's food and drinking cups of hot chocolate and chatting until the early hours of the morning. There was such a huge sense of community.

The power is still out, but I have never been happier (excluding my wedding day, of course). We have made some real friends tonight and I certainly count Annie as one of them.
  Jake

Sunday:
The power is back on, just in time to cook breakfast. I'm not sure eggs and baked beans would be easy to cook on a barbeque.

I think I might be pregnant. It's so early in our marriage and I wanted time alone with Jake before we had kids.

We have spoken about it though. Jake would like a whole football team.

What??!! You write this in the book and don't tell me first!?

Monday:
I'm not pregnant. Though I wanted more time, I can't help feeling a huge sense of disappointment. I had already started to think about names. ☹

My darling Rosie, there's plenty of time yet. I love you and we have the rest of our lives together.

Till next time, Annie.
  Jake x

❧

2nd to 6th May
Phil and Sue Martin

We have had a lovely time here in Wells-Next-The-Sea. Our dog Jack loved the beach so much, he had to be carried off it at the end of the day. Not an easy feat considering how big he is. Willow Cottage is delightful. The Frog and Rhubarb does fantastic food and even lets in dogs, which was great for us.
  Phil, Sue and Jack the dog.

❧

10th May to ?
Barney Quinn

Saturday:
Although I am here as a guest, I will soon be a permanent resident of Chalk Hill. My new house, aptly named The Sandcastle for its yellow colouring, is just going under some much-needed renovations. I'm staying here to oversee and help with its upgrade before I move in a few weeks from now.

I've not met the landlady of this lovely cottage yet. Though I spoke with Annie Butterworth on the phone, she was not here to meet me. Apparently there was some problem with her painting studio and Sophia Lorenzo let me in instead.

The local villagers I've met so far seem to be so friendly and so willing to help. I even had an offer to see some cows from some man called William. Not wishing to offend him, I accepted and spent a rather dull hour listening to him talk about them as I watched them graze.

I would like to say a huge thank you, Annie, for the books, maps and leaflets of the local area that you left for me. This will be a huge help in the coming weeks.

My temporary next-door neighbour is beautiful. I've just seen her in her back garden chasing the chickens back into their pens. This must be Annie's granddaughter.

Would it be considered bad form to date the granddaughter of your landlady? I can't take my eyes off her. God, that arse.

Have just met the blonde vision. She's called Annie too, probably after her grandmother. Annie wanted to know if I had settled in all right, so I imagine she handles the cottage when her grandmother isn't here. I'm going to ensure all my dealings are with the young Annie from now on. She is lovely. The dress she was wearing was slightly see-through in the sunlight and showed off her legs beautifully. Shame about the big sandals, kind of ruined the image a bit, but at least she wasn't wearing them with socks. I've asked her to drop round fresh eggs every day.

Have just bought supplies from the village shop. Local milk, local bread, local cider, local cheese, local butter and local meat, so said the very elderly lady as she served me. Not local condoms though. She thought this was very funny. She was still cackling at her little joke when I left the shop.

Sunday:
Last day of rest today before the builders descend tomorrow. I'll ask Annie to join me for a picnic on the beach. Will pack all the local produce for lunch. And non-local produce for dessert!! Well, just in case.

Just dropping eggs off. There seems to be a bit of confusion. I am the Annie Butterworth you spoke with on the phone, I own Willow Cottage. The only living grandmother I have is called Cerise and lives in France.

Thanks for the comments about my bum and legs, very much appreciated. I'm glad you are making the most of the local produce and the non-local. It is always good to be prepared!!

A picnic sounds lovely. I'll bring the chocolate-chip cheese-cake I made this morning for dessert. Much tastier than eating condoms, they can be a bit rubbery!!

Have never blushed so much in my entire life. Annie couldn't stop laughing about it. She has the loveliest laugh I've ever heard.

Picnic was lovely. We talked a lot. Annie is very funny and sweet. I get the sense she was holding something back from me. She's been hurt in the past, some cheating ex-boyfriend scum most likely. We're taking things slow for now.

Monday:
Urgh, the builders have arrived across the green at some ungodly hour. Better go and make tea and supervise the extension and new fitted kitchen.

Despite the fact that I have found the best builders money can buy, and despite the fact that I have paid them extra to have this job finished quicker, they still stand around a lot and drink tea. They took an hour and half for lunch and haven't brought all the parts/tools they need today.

My day has just got one million per cent better. I have just seen Annie naked. Oh my god! She is beautiful. She has a tiny mole on her bum and a scar across her shoulder, but she is perfect in every single way.

I perhaps should add why I saw her naked, I'm not a sleazy peeping tom. There was a fox in her garden and Annie saw him just as she was getting out the shower. Without a moment's hesitation she ran downstairs and out into the garden to scare him off before he could eat the chickens. I, of course, ran round to help too, though the fox had already gone by then. Annie was a little embarrassed to have me see her naked, but she still had the good grace to invite me round for dinner. I did ask what the dress code was and whether

I should come as casually as she was dressed. She said maybe I should wear a tie. Sorely tempted to turn up just wearing a tie, but need to remember we're taking things slow.

Tuesday:
A great evening with Annie, she makes me laugh a lot.

Just dropping off fresh towels. I had a lovely evening too. I'll be at the painting studio all day today until quite late tonight but maybe we can do it again on Thursday.

I would love to.

The builders have made good progress today, despite their continual tea breaks.

Wednesday:
Hi, Barney. I'm Sophia, the cleaner, we met on Saturday. I normally pop by once a week to tidy things up, but we've not had any long-term residents before. If you would prefer to be left alone, rather than me coming in and disturbing you, then please let me or Annie know.

Annie is walking around with a huge grin on her face about her dates with you. I haven't seen her this excited and happy for a long, long time. She's had a difficult few years, so just be careful with her. Be patient, and I promise you it will be worth it. She is a lovely girl with a beautiful heart.

I've just been told off for writing this, apparently she doesn't want you to know about her past so I'll say no more about it. Though quite how she expects to keep it quiet in Chalk Hill is beyond me.

I am not made out of china; I do not need to be treated as such.

Though I do appreciate you're only looking out for me.

Everyone has baggage, Sophia, I'm sure Annie's is no worse than anyone else's. If she doesn't want to talk about it, then I won't push her or anyone else for information. We are taking things slow and, as I am moving into Chalk Hill permanently, I have no intention of hurting her or treating her badly. I would be a fool to, not least because I'd then have to face the wrath of you and the other twelve villagers that have already warned me off her.
  Barney

I'm sorry the villagers have felt the need to speak to you about me. They're very protective. I promise you I don't have any foul or hideous diseases. But if you want to call it off, I'd completely understand.
  Annie x

Glad to hear of your good health! I'm very much looking forward to dinner tomorrow night. Even villagers with their pitchforks wouldn't stop me.

Thursday:
With an extra cash bonus hanging on the end of a stick for the builders if they finish it all by the end of next week, they are now working like trojans. They are still going through more teabags than I've had hot dinners, but at least now they are drinking whilst they work.

Had a lovely dinner again tonight with Annie, drank a few bottles of local cider and then a very disappointing walk on the beach. It couldn't have been more romantic with the moon shining over the water, but we still haven't kissed yet. It's so frustrating. I know I said we were taking it slow, but at the moment we aren't even moving.

Friday:
Just popping some eggs in. I'm sorry you were disappointed with last night. There are quite a few single girls in the village and surrounding areas who would be more than willing to move quicker. You'd probably be better off with one of them.
  Annie

My lovely Annie. Please don't get upset by my slightly drunken ramblings, that cider is potent stuff. I don't want any other girl, I only want you. I suppose I thought that if we hadn't even kissed yet then what I really want to be doing with you was a very, very long way off. I'm happy to wait, but I don't want to just be friends with you, I want more, much more. If you don't see us going that way, then I'd rather know now.

Just got back from a day at the house, the kitchen is nearly done and the foundations are finished for the extension.

No word from Annie, I'd better keep an eye out for angry villagers with burning torches.

Saturday:
I like you, Barney, I really do, and definitely more than just as friends. I'm just not sure I'm ready for a relationship yet. This is all so new for me and, quite honestly, more than a bit scary.

Just got back from a run. I don't want to rush you, Annie, I've got all the time in the world. I'm heading over to the house now, the builders are putting in half a day today. I'd love to have you over for dinner tonight. No cider this time though.

Annie's coming for dinner tonight, what on earth do I cook for someone who is such a brilliant cook herself? My talents lie firmly in the 'something on toast' department. Maybe a takeaway is the answer. I can spend more time chatting with her then.

Feel like such a shit. Had another wonderful evening with Annie, but she finally told me why she was holding back. There was me thinking she'd just had a crappy ex-boyfriend. not that her husband, her childhood sweetheart, had died two years ago. No wonder she is hesitant to take the next step. She must feel guilty for moving on and concerned for what the villagers will think, especially his family who live here too.

Sunday:
Please don't feel bad. That's exactly why I didn't tell you. I have enough pity from the locals without you joining in too. It was nice to be treated normally for a while. Though I felt like I owed you an explanation for my reticence, which is why I told you.

I don't feel guilty for moving on. My life shouldn't stop just because Nick's did. And I'm not concerned about what people will think. They can think what they like. Most of them will be happy for me and those that aren't, I don't care about anyway.

Nick's family will be supportive too. They wouldn't expect me to sit in mourning for the rest of my life. No, the reason

I'm holding back is purely the thought of being with someone that isn't Nick. It feels very weird.

Knock on my back door when you wake up, maybe we can go for a drive.

What a fantastic day. Thought it was time to see that beautiful smile back on Annie's face, so we drove down to Great Yarmouth and went to the pleasure beach. We spent the day riding the rollercoasters, racing each other on the go-karts and eating candy floss and fish and chips on the pier. The highlight for me was her grabbing me in the Haunted Hotel.

Ha ha! I was holding you because you were clearly scared, I was offering comfort. I had the best time today, thank you so much.

Mmm, finally a kiss!!

Monday:
The builders arrived at seven this morning, obviously they are keen to get this cash bonus.

Tuesday:
Barney, I've just taken a last-minute enquiry for half term next week, do you think you'll be out by then? No worries if not.

Yes, I should be. The house is starting to look amazing. There are a few things here and there that need to be finished, but I'm keen to move in now as soon as possible. I'm going to move in on Friday so I'll be out of your hair then.

I would love you to come over and see it. I'll make you

dinner Saturday night in my new kitchen and if travelling back across the green is too far for you, you could always stay over afterwards.

Dinner will be lovely, though I think I can manage to find my way back across the green again.

Well, if you're sure, I'd hate for you to get lost.

I'll think about it.

Wednesday:
I'm off to buy new bedding for my king-size bed, can't wait to sleep in it on Friday in my new home and hopefully christen it on Saturday.

Barney, can I just remind you, you're supposed to be taking things slow.
   Sophia Lorenzo

Sophia!!! I'm more than capable of saying no if I'm not ready.

And, Barney, please don't write things like that in the guest-book, other people will read it after you've gone.

Sorry. Barney x

Me too. I worry about you, that's all. I'm sure Olly would be worried too, if he knew.

Which is why he doesn't need to know. Olly would have me dressed in black and mourning his brother for the rest of my life. Is that what you want too?

No, of course not, I'm pleased that you're having fun, really I am. I just don't want to see you getting hurt or rushing into anything you're not sure about. I love you and if you're happy, then I'm happy. Sophia x

And, Barney, if you hurt her, I'll have your testicles on a plate.

Duly noted.

Sophia, you do make me laugh. I'd be quite proficient at serving Barney's testicles on a plate myself if it comes to that, I am a culinary queen, after all.

Erm, feeling quite nervous about the safety of my testicles now. Maybe Sophia would like to chaperone our dinner on Saturday and escort you back safely across the green afterwards. Therefore your chastity and my testicles remain intact.

That won't be necessary.

Thursday:
Have spent a very long day unpacking boxes and cleaning in an attempt to make my house a home. Exhausted. I've just got back here very late to find a chicken pie freshly cooked and just in need of reheating for my dinner. Annie, I may actually be a little bit in love with you.

Friday:
Thanks so much for your hospitality over the last two weeks. I'm looking forward to our dinner tomorrow night, with or without the dessert.

24th to 31st May
Gemma, Sean and Charlie Chadwick

Saturday:

My maternity leave is coming to a close. Next week, after half term, I return to the classroom. I haven't been a teacher for a year now, since Charlie was born and I've enjoyed just being a mum. He has grown so much and I will miss not spending every day with him. Though I am looking forward to having my brain filled with other things rather than dirty nappies, poo explosions and nursery rhymes. Thankfully all the children I'll be working with are toilet-trained and have long since out-grown nursery rhymes. They're more bothered about who's dating who and whether Harry Styles is fitter than Justin Bieber.

The weather is forecast to stay nice, at least for the next few days, so we'll be enjoying the beach and spending the last bit of family time together. Next week I'll be up to my eyeballs in marking and meetings and Charlie will be spending his days split between his grandparents and nursery.

Gemma Chadwick

Monday:

It's the very early hours of Monday morning now. Charlie has been awake all the night; he's either teething or coming down with a cold. With nothing to do but comfort him, I've been reading this book. It makes for a gripping read.

Annie, I can't believe your brother-in-law is Oliver Black. I love him. His books and films aren't bad either. Sean is completely in love with him as well, though apparently it's more an appreciation for his work than for his body. I think it's a man crush!!! Sean follows his progress more avidly in the gossip mags than I do.

I have to ask you, why are you not with him? It's clear from his messages in this book that he has a thing for you. I've not seen this Barney, but surely he can't compare to the great Oliver Black? And you probably won't answer this, but did you stay over with Barney on Saturday night?

Tuesday:
Yes, the guestbook has taken off in ways I never expected. It seems that not having the pressure of talking face to face means that people can put what they really feel in this book.

Oliver and I are good friends. We have been since we were little. What you perceive as him having a thing for me is nothing more than a fondness from him. He sees me as a little sister, especially since I married his brother. Since Nick died, Olly has looked out for me, but being with him is not an option. I'm sure you know from the gossip mags that Oliver has been engaged to the beautiful actress Vivienne Lake for over two years.

As for Barney, he has been sweet, patient and a lot of fun to be with. Plus he's very fit too. We had a nice time Saturday night, though I'll say no more about it.

Curses! And you and I both know that the thing with Vivienne Lake is a complete farce. I have very close female friends, but none of them are as close as Vivienne and her 'best friend' Darcy. If this thing between Vivienne and Oliver is real, then he is either blind to the fact that his girlfriend is gay or maybe he's OK with it and one of those men that likes to watch.

Wednesday:
As far as I know, Oliver and Vivienne are very much in love

with each other. You shouldn't believe everything that you read in the papers. Oliver is a lovely bloke and the papers always make him out to be a complete tart; it simply isn't true.

Spoken like someone who is completely in love with him.

Although comments in the papers can be taken with a pinch of salt, photos don't lie. For months, after your husband died, you and Oliver were pictured walking hand in hand along the beach. He stayed in your house every night. Don't tell me that nothing happened between you. Many critics believe this 'relationship' with Vivienne was Oliver's attempt to get the press to leave you alone.

Nothing happened. We're friends, that's it. When Nick died, I fell apart, Oliver stayed to help pick up the pieces.

Gemma, you are a guest in Annie's house. Just because you have paid for a week's accommodation doesn't give you the right to give her the third degree about her private life or to be bitchy about her or Oliver.
Sophia Lorenzo, cleaner

It's fine, Sophia. People will always be interested in Oliver Black. Wells-Next-The-Sea and the people he grew up with will naturally be of interest too. People will make their own minds up about him with or without my help.

My apologies if my comments hurt you, that wasn't my intention. My brain has become addled with worthless gossip since I've been on maternity leave and living next door to you for a week and therefore Oliver Black by proxy, is the most exciting thing that has ever happened to me.

Apart from getting married and giving birth to Charlie, of

course. Apologies, Annie, my wife is not normally this blood-thirsty for inane gossip. Sitting at home with Charlie all day has sent her doolally. Your house is lovely and we are having a lovely time enjoying the beach.

Sean Chadwick

Thursday:
Speaking of Oliver Black, he has made it back into gossip magazine *Purple Moon* again. He and Vivienne were seen having a row in Covent Garden last week. Seems the 'very much in love' couple are not quite as in love as you thought.

Sorry, I'm at it again.

Friday:
I'm determined my last few messages are going to be gossip-free. Charlie is loving the beach; he loves the waves and paddling in the shallows. He loves the sand, so much he even tries to eat it.

Have just seen Annie with a very huge, very fit man out on the green. I'm guessing this is Barney. They looked very much together, so I guess she did sleep with him on Saturday.

Sorry, I just can't seem to stop.

Saturday:
Thanks, Annie, we've had a great week. Good luck with the whole Barney/Oliver debacle. It's been brilliant to get the inside scoop.

I'm so glad my life has entertained you.

31st May to 2nd June
Jacqualyn, Mark and Alfie Rumsey

A lovely weekend planned with my favourite boys.
  Jac Rumsey

I think we were supposed to be booked in for last weekend, over the bank holiday, but I think Mark got the dates mixed up. He assures me he meant to book this weekend all along. I'm on maternity leave with Alfie, so it doesn't affect me, but he's had to book a day off work now.

My husband has left the sling at home.

And the baby formula.

And the changing bag.

Ha, and his own clothes.

You said you had packed the car.

With the stuff that you put by the door. You said that was everything.

Keith has said he'll bring up the rest of our stuff, kip on our sofa and drive back tomorrow.

Good for you, or you'd be driving back to collect it.

Just popped by to see if you're all settled in. I'll make up the spare bedroom for your friend Keith; I wouldn't want him to sleep on the sofa. Michael and Shellie Atkinson at number twelve have a child about six months older than Alfie. They have kept all the stuff in case they have a second child. I'm sure they wouldn't mind lending it to you for the duration of your stay, might save Keith the journey. I will ask them for you. Though I can't do anything about Mark's clothes.

Annie x

Thanks, Annie. We've just got back from a walk and Keith is already on his way. If he leaves any baby stuff behind, we'll let you know and we'll borrow what we need from the Atkinsons. If he leaves Mark's clothes behind, we may have to steal some clothes from the scarecrow in the field.

Jac

Oooh, naked scarecrows, interesting.

Keith to the rescue once more. I've brought everything that you asked me to and locked the kitchen window as it was left open. I turned the iron off as that was still on and threw away a very mouldy loaf of bread.

Keith

MARK!!!!!

Sunday:

Breakfast *à la* Jac. I hope Mark forgets his stuff more often if I get rewarded like this. I'm sticking around for a morning on the beach with my godson and the famous Rumsey Roast this afternoon, then I'll be making my way back home.

Keith

Thanks, boyo. Have you seen my iPhone, it seems to have gone missing.
Mark

Monday:
I really do love my husband. He took Alfie out for a walk this morning so I could sleep in and even brought me breakfast in bed.

We've had a lovely weekend. The Frog and Rhubarb has amazing food.
Thanks, Annie.

❧

6th to 8th June
Max, Jade, Lottie and Oz

We are diving down at Blakeney and Cley tomorrow. So a few beers tonight down the Frog before our very early start in the morning to catch low tide.
Max

The diving here is quite spectacular, some of the deeper dives further off shore are amazing, but as Lottie and Oz are relatively new to the sport we are keeping to some of the shallower dives this weekend. The vis would be better in the autumn when the water is cooler, but still it should be a good dive.
Jade

And the beers are an integral part to any diving weekend.
Oz

Saturday:
  Urgh, it's so early.

Lottie, welcome to the life of a diver, we are ruled by the tides.
  Max

But why do the tides have to be so early?

It'll totally be worth it. Your first sea dive, are you excited?
  Jade

A bit scared but, yes, very excited.

We will take care of you, besides, all the dives this weekend are very shallow. Nothing will go wrong, I promise. Now, go and get your boyfriend out of bed.

We've just got back from diving *The Vera*, quick bite of lunch before we head out to catch the afternoon's low tide on *The Amberley*.
  ***The Vera* was amazing, so much sea life. It collided and sank in 1915 and the tides have broken it up quite badly, but it's shallow enough to get some amazing photos. There were crabs, dead men's fingers and loads of anemones. Also tonnes of bass, too.**
  Oz

I'm so glad Jade told me to bring cocktail sausages with us on the dive; hand-feeding the bass was so fantastic. Max and Jade stayed close to us, but it helped that I could still see the surface throughout the dive.
  Lottie

Pipefish, sunstars, crystal sea slugs; what a great dive! The newbies did very well on their first sea dive. Took some excellent photos of the rib cage of *The Vera*.

Jade

Come on, *The Amberley* is a-calling. Your first dive from a boat, should be interesting.

Max

Sunday:
We got back late last night. After the huge buzz of diving on *The Amberley*, we hit the pub to celebrate. We missed low tide this morning on *The Rosalie*, but caught it this afternoon for another spectacular dive. I could get used to this. Bloody freezing though, even in our drysuits.

Oz

20th to 23rd June
Verity Forbes

I would prefer to be called by my full name, Verity the Voyeur.

Erm, OK.

I am here because Norfolk has lots of ghost stories associated with its history; sailors from the past that have crashed onto these shores, Victorians, Stuarts, Tudors, I can feel them all. Chalk Hill is built on the crossing of several ley lines and because of this it becomes a gathering of trapped spirits.

With the summer solstice this weekend, spiritual activity will be at its highest.

My spirit guide, Arron Davenport, has told me that the village green, in particular, will be the place to meet some of these characters from the past. I can't wait to get started.

I feel I should explain more about Arron Davenport, I don't want to come across as a mad woman. Arron was a captain of the seventeenth-century frigate, The Grey Horse, who explored the cold northern countries for King Charles. He wasn't very successful. On his first outing he crashed the boat on some rocks and the entire crew were drowned. Arron has since told me that his heart lay in farming and he only became a sailor because his father was before him. His father was also killed at sea, when he accidentally fired a cannon on his own ship and the boat sank without trace. Records are not clear on how he managed to fire a cannon at his own ship, but clearly the Davenports were not that skilled in the sailing department. I found Arron when I was doing a séance; he spoke to me and, although we don't get on all that well, we have become good companions.

Arron is not happy that I have been insulting his skills as a sailor. But the facts are a matter of public record.

I'm going for a walk now to get a feel for the area before tomorrow's big ceremony.

Annie, do you know if I will be allowed to light a fire on the village green?

We have had barbeques and fires on the green before, so I don't see why not. We are quite laidback here; most people will barely bat an eyelid.
Annie x

That's good.

Just got back from my walk. The place is buzzing with psychic energy. There are so many ghosts here. I'm going to hold a séance on the village green later to see if I can communicate with any of them.

There were three spirits I spoke with tonight; one especially was concerned about an engagement ring that was found on the beach. She wants it returned to the sea where the bodies of her and her lover lie buried beneath the sands. Annie, do you know of this engagement ring? If you have it, you can give it to me and I will return it to its rightful owners.

Do you know a Mary? She was one of the spirits that spoke to me last night, she seemed to know you.

Saturday:
The only Mary I know is Mary Gillespie, who is alive and kicking and lives on the other side of the green.

Marie then, or May, or Myra? Sometimes the names don't come through that clearly.

No, sorry.

Well, anyway, Mary said that you had to make a tough decision, but you knew in your heart what the right choice was.

I knew it. Cheese on toast for lunch it is then.

Please don't be scathing about my gift.

My apologies. It wasn't my wish to cause offence. I expect lots of people are having to face a hard decision of some kind at the moment, maybe Mary wanted to speak to one of those. It seems odd that someone I don't know would try to leave me a message.

I admit it might seem strange, but the spirit world does work in mysterious ways. It is not my place to question these messages. I am merely a conduit to receive them and pass them on.

Did Mary say anything else?

She said that it was hidden in the biscuit tin.

Right. I'll bear that in mind.

The third spirit was more interested in Arron than in talking to me. They spoke about hidden treasure and smuggling. Fascinating stuff really, what could be buried right under our noses.

I need to prepare for the celebrations tonight. Feel free to join me on the green later for the solstice.

I'll certainly be happy to watch for a while.

I have the candles, the harp and the crystals. I'm very much looking forward to tonight. I just hope the villagers will embrace it and not mock it. The more the merrier.

Sunday:

Verity, I just came by to see if you were OK after last night. The summer solstice rituals were very interesting and I think many of the villagers would have watched it longer or even joined in, though I don't think anyone was really prepared for when you stripped naked and danced around the fire. The harp music was beautiful and all the crystals hanging from the trees looked magical. The dancing was... lovely. I think the men of the village especially loved the shaking part. I know you had dressed up for the occasion; it was such a shame that the gold body paint and hair spray was so flammable. Thank god for the quick thinking of Gary from the darts team who decided leaping on you and rolling you in the grass would put the fire out. It's a shame that he rolled you into the pond, but that was probably for the best; it did wash off all the duck poo that he had rolled you in after all. You didn't seem to have any scarring, Gary seemed quite thorough in checking you over, but I've left you some Savlon just in case.

I was so embarrassed. I'm trying to present a professional front to the spirits on the one night of the year that more spirits can pass through to this world, and I ended up looking like a drowned rat. Arron thought it was hilarious, he said it was the funniest thing he has seen in the last three hundred and eighty-four years. Gary was very sweet about it all.

I don't think you looked like a drowned rat, I thought you looked adorable.
   Gary

Oh... Hi, Gary, I didn't realise you were still here.

I was quite shaken up last night, Gary stayed with me to make sure I was OK.

Thanks for the Savlon, Annie, I'll make sure it gets rubbed into some of Verity's sorer parts.

Erm... I'll leave you to it.

Monday:
Had a lovely, unexpectedly fantastic weekend. I may see you again soon. Don't forget to check the biscuit tin.

So, now she's gone, I have to ask, what was in the biscuit tin?

Oh, Sophia, something wonderful, something amazing.

Custard Creams?

Yes, and something else.

Milk chocolate digestives?

You know me so well.

Do you not think you should have your customers certifiably checked over by a psychiatrist before you allow them to stay?

Why? It makes life more interesting.

I must admit that I have never laughed so hard in my entire life as when Gary was trying to give her mouth to mouth when she was clearly still alive and kicking. And her harp playing wasn't what I'd class as music.

No, bless her, she might have many gifts but musical ability is not one of them.

Gary seemed very impressed with the gifts she did have though.

Very impressed. I thought the groans and shouts I heard on Saturday night and last night were her chants to the dead, but on hindsight I gather they were something else.

⚘

28th June to 5th July
~~Vivienne Lake~~ Penelope Pitstop

Hi, Penelope. Just to let you know, I won't be here after Tuesday. I'm going to stay with my friend Hetty in Tenby for a week or so before the peak season hits. Apparently she has a rather lovely gardener called Connor that I really need to meet!!! After you I don't have another booking till late July, so I'm going to make the most of it.

    Sophia Lorenzo lives at number three, the pink cottage across the green, she will be around if there are any problems.

    I know your friend will be joining you later on in the week. I presume you don't want the other bedroom made up?

    Annie x

Aw, Annie, Penelope Pitstop? Couldn't I be Jessica Rabbit instead?

    Viv x

And no, one bed will be fine.

You certainly have the figure to be Jessica Rabbit, but Penelope Pitstop has those great white boots and the funky car, besides she has spirit. Jessica Rabbit is underhanded and deceitful.

Fair point. I'm looking forward to a long week of relaxation. I haven't stopped for the past eighteen months. Filming Behind Closed Doors has been so much fun but exhausting.

Just be thankful Olly wasn't directing or producing his own book, it would have taken five years for him to be happy with the final result.

He is a perfectionist.

And he's going out with you?

Haha! You do make me laugh, Annie. It's good to see you again.

How are things between you two anyway?

In front of the camera or behind? Away from the press we're getting on fine, he makes me laugh though he's obviously not my type!! In front of the cameras, for the sake of the paparazzi, things between me and The Great Oliver Black are starting to become a bit strained. The paps do love a bit of drama. Though, to be honest, the strain from him is more real than I'd like. The man needs to get laid, he hasn't been with a woman for over two years.

Two years, really?

Yeah ever since... shit, sorry, Annie, how insensitive of me.

Don't sweat it. Come for dinner tonight, instead of me communicating through this book every time I walk past it in my attempts to fix the bloomin' washing machine. I may have to seriously think about a plumber. There's only so much my dear old dad passed onto me before he died.

No, don't get a plumber. I was enjoying watching you come in dressed in those overalls. ;-)

My apologies, I didn't realise I had walked into some dodgy Eighties porno.

Haha! Dinner sounds lovely. Now, I'd better get back to writing my autobiography. As if anyone will be interested in my life story! I'm only twenty-five, I've not really had any life to speak of yet.

Except being a famous Hollywood starlet since the age of six.

Oh yes, that.

Sunday:
Have had the longest lie-in since as far back as I can remember. Woke just after lunch and that was only because I was ravenous and could smell bacon cooking from below. Stumble downstairs to find Annie serving up a huge breakfast in my kitchen. If she wasn't already spoken for, I would marry her on the spot.

Sod Olly, finder's keepers. I'm taking Annie to Gretna

Green, we shall be married by the end of the day. That will give the press something to talk about. Brunch was the best I've ever tasted.

Just texted Olly to ask his advice on writing. My auto-biography is boring me and it's my story! His advice was to embellish, lie and exaggerate wherever possible and only use a smattering of truth. And if my story is really that dull, kill off a few key players; that always keeps the readers on their toes. I like the idea of embellishment, but I think killing off Johnny Depp and George Clooney might be going a bit too far.

He's just texted me again to say that I should write the bit about breaking up with him and how bereft it made me feel. He's right, by the time this book hits the shelves, it will be over between us. Need to find the right words to describe my heartbreak. Inconsolable, distraught, grief-stricken. Haha! He's right, writing that bit should be fun. Completely inaccurate but fun.

I'm going to have to glue these pages together once you've gone. You're giving too much away. Other people will read this, you know.

I'm Penelope Pitstop. They're not going to be interested in little old me.

Hmmm >:-(

OK, OK, I'll speak in code from now on.

The blue cow flies east in the winter.

Code only works if the other person knows the code.

Spoilsport.

The black crow has green eyes.

OK, that's one I understand.

Monday:
OK, Annie, I have a story of my own, maybe you can help me with the ending.

The black crow and the magpie were brothers. They grew up together, did everything together. Often on their adventures they were joined by a pale gold dove.

The dove was beautiful and, as they all grew up together, the magpie and the crow tried different ways to impress the dove, hoping to be the one to win the dove's heart. It seemed, however, that the dove was in love with them both, that there could never be a choice between them.

The black crow yearned to be free of the tiny wood in which he lived, whereas the magpie was happy to stay where he was, to raise his own tiny magpies there one day. This would ultimately be the decider for the gold dove.

The dove had dreams of freedom too, but she'd not had the happiest childhood. The dove's mother had been in and out of her life frequently as the dove grew up. Often the dove's mother would leave for weeks or months at a time, never with any form of contact whilst she was away. When the dove was sixteen, her mother disappeared again, this time, never to return.

The crow recognised that the dove needed stability and that he could never give her that. He was young and impetuous. He drank and smoked and sometimes when the dove was with him she smoked too. She was young and innocent and he wanted her to stay that way. He knew that, with him, she would only end up going down a dark path. He bored easily and the thought of settling in one place for the rest of his life scared him. He wanted to travel the world and never put down roots. He knew that if he asked the dove to come with him, she probably would but that she would miss out on the constancy and permanence she so desperately needed.

The crow knew his brother, the magpie, loved the dove as much as he did and he couldn't bear to hurt his brother by taking the dove with him. So the crow left the tiny wood to seek his fortune in the wider world, leaving the dove in the safe, protective ~~hands~~ wings of his younger brother.

When the crow returned, as he had foreseen, the magpie and the dove were happily married and, apart from the huge ache in his heart, the crow knew all was right with the world.

For five long years, the magpie and dove lived their happily-ever-afters, completely in love, whilst the crow travelled the world, made lots of friends and tried to forget where his heart lay by spending time with lots of other very pretty female birds.

Then disaster struck. One cold winter, when the crow was back in the tiny wood visiting his brother and the dove, there was a horrible accident which ended the life of the magpie.

Instead of returning to his life of fun and frolics after the funeral, the crow stayed to tend to the broken heart of the dove. He knew that he would willingly give up that life to stay by the dove's side for ever. He loved her, had always loved her, and wherever she was would now be his home. It seemed that the dove returned these feelings, that being married to his brother had never diminished the love she felt for him.

Suddenly, just seven months after the death of the magpie, the crow fled back to his former life. Though he still loved the dove and the dove loved him, there seemed to be something holding the young lovebirds back.

It is now two years after the magpie has died and the lovebirds are still unable to take that final step. Will they ever be together or are they destined to live their lives alone, never filling the gap that has been left in their hearts?

Shit, Annie, I'm sorry, I never meant to make you cry.

Tuesday:
I feel awful. I'm so sorry, Annie, I didn't mean to hurt you. Please answer your door.

I've been at The Painted Plate all day today, my pottery painting studio. I'm fine. I'm having an early night as I'm getting up early tomorrow to drive to Tenby so I probably won't see you again before you leave. Take care.
  Annie x

You're obviously not fine. Look, one night me and Olly got really drunk and he told me everything. I thought you knew all this, that he loves you completely and always has. I thought the only thing holding you back was that you weren't ready after Nick died. But then I read this thing with Barney and that you are going off to play with some fit gardener called Connor and it's clear you are ready to move on now, but why aren't you moving on with Olly?

Olly does not love me. Whatever drunken ramblings he uttered to you that night were just that, ramblings.

When we were younger, he always spoke about leaving, that he wanted to see the world. Just like my mum. When he was eighteen, he booked his ticket to the States. I begged him not to go, told him I loved him in the hope that, if he had something to stay for, he wouldn't go. But I wasn't enough. I needed him in my life and, with him gone, it felt like half my heart had been ripped out. But the other half of my heart belonged to Nick. I love them both, always have and always will. But Olly was wrong. Though I yearned for freedom, I could never have left my dad behind, not after Mum had left. I couldn't bear to leave Nick either. If there was a choice between him and Olly, I could never have made it. As it happens, I didn't need to. Olly didn't feel for me what I felt for him and he left.

After Nick died, Olly stayed with me for nearly seven months, slept in the bed with me, holding me as I cried myself to sleep. Of course nothing happened between us. I wasn't in any fit state. I know the press were slating him for jumping straight into the marital bed before it had even gone cold. There were pictures in the papers of us holding hands on the beach, or him with his arm round me. But it wasn't like that between us.

Until the night before he left. We got drunk, we slept together and the next day he ran. We didn't speak for six months. Seemingly he was engaged to you, had been since before

Nick had died. I thought for a while that that was why he ran, he felt guilty for cheating on you, or that your patience with the grieving widow had finally run out. It wasn't until I met you that I realised it was all a sham. But if he didn't run because of you, then he ran because he doesn't want me. It was pity sex, pure and simple. Grief sex at best.

So your story, as nice as it is, is nothing more than a fairy tale.

And I'm definitely gluing these pages together after you've gone.

Wednesday:
Damn it. I can't believe you snuck in last night and wrote all this and now you've already gone. We need to talk about this. Though actually the person you really need to speak to is Olly. The stupid man should have told you how he felt and why he ran.

My guilt has been pushed aside slightly with the arrival of the beautiful Darcy Burbridge.

Viv, Penelope, whichever name you are going under, you are so indiscreet. You were the one that wanted to keep our relationship secret. You were the one that said the British public weren't ready for their national treasure to be gay. Olly has gone to a lot of trouble to help you in this charade and then you spill all his innermost secrets, and most of ours, in this book. If you want people to know, I'll go outside and shout it from the rooftops right now.

Darcy, don't be mad. I missed you and the secrecy is driving me mad.

Me too, but I'm not about to drag Olly and Annie down with us. When the time is right, Olly will dump you and you can seek solace with me, as we planned. Not before. And I'll glue these pages together myself before we leave.

Thursday:
Annie, thank you so much for letting me stay. There are literally no places in the world that we are safe to be seen together without being hounded by the press. They know I'm Viv's best friend, but if we are seen together in hotels then people will soon start to be suspicious. Hotel staff are the most indiscreet and word would soon get out. I feel safe here, safe to finally be with the woman I love.

Your neighbours are fiercely loyal to you and, as such, loyal to us too. No one cares who we are and the press will never find us here.

I'm sorry if this sham between Viv and Olly brings you any grief, or if Viv has hurt you in any way with her flapping mouth. I've met Olly quite a few times, stayed with him in his house in New York. Viv speaks the truth. He's crazy about you, that much is clear. He has photos of you everywhere, even on the screensaver of his laptop. I'm sorry that you have to find out through me or Viv and not from the silly man himself.

Darcy X

Friday:
A lovely day at the beach today. We stayed mainly in the dunes, it was very quiet and romantic.

I still feel wracked with guilt. Annie, you're the last person in the world I'd want to hurt. I'm not even sure how I did it. Surely finding out that Olly loves you is a good thing. He loves you, you love him, butterbing, butterboom!

Saturday:
We're leaving today. Thanks so much for your hospitality.

You probably won't thank me for this either, but I told Olly what I had done. He was furious. I think he might be on his way over.
 Hope it all works out for you.
 Viv x

❧

7th July to–?
Oliver Black

Monday:
I've just arrived from New York to talk to Annie, only to find she's not here. Sophia let me in, reluctantly, and I'm staying until Annie gets back.

At least without Annie knocking on my door every few minutes, I'll be able to get some writing done until she comes home.

Tuesday:
The last time I was here, I persuaded Annie to use Twitter. I thought it might be another way to get Willow Cottage noticed if she was posting special offers and what was going on in the local area. She agreed to give it a go for herself first and

once she got the hang of it she would open a Twitter account under the name of Willow Cottage. I set up an account for her and showed her how to use it.

This has backfired spectacularly on me. As one of her few followers, I'm now being updated with progress on her holiday. Tweets like 'Went to the beach with Connor today' and 'Connor is the most beautiful man I've ever seen' and 'Connor and I are going on a trip to Skomer Island' and 'I may actually be in love' are pissing me right off.

I've phoned and tweeted her, but she hasn't replied. She seems to be deliberately ignoring me.

Wednesday:
Annie, did Vivienne mention the money, is that why you're angry with me?

I had to give you the money. Without Nick's income you would never have been able to afford the mortgage repayments on your home and on Willow Cottage. Of course he wasn't insured, I only told you that so you'd accept the money. Even if he was, what kind of insurance policy do you think would pay out two million pounds?

I had to know you would be OK, with everything else that was going on I didn't want money to be an issue for you. And, after all, it's my fault that he's dead. You've never said as much, but you must think it. I was driving the car. I should have done something, reacted quicker, anything to avoid the other car.

Thursday:
I am furious. Sally Jenkins, another one of Annie's followers, has tweeted demanding to know details about Connor. Annie has replied that he is magnificent in *every single way* possible.

I'm so livid, Annie. I didn't give you all that money so you could spend it jumping into bed with any man who catches your eye. First me, then Barney and now Connor. You're not the person I thought you were. Did Nick mean nothing to you? And what kind of stupid ass name is Barney? Sounds like a sodding dinosaur.

I've just split open Vivienne and Darcy's entries. I can't believe you say you loved me the whole time you were married to Nick. Do you know how sick that makes me? Do you have no loyalty at all? How do you think Nick would feel if he knew that?

I'm going to keep ringing you until you answer.

Friday:
If I knew where Hetty lived, I'd drive up there and drag you home myself.

What happened between us that night was a mistake. It will never happen again. I at least have some integrity over honouring my brother's memory, where you appear to have none.

Saturday:
I have just texted and left an answerphone message for Annie to say there's been a fire at Willow Cottage. She phoned me straight back and I told her she needed to come home as soon as she could.

I'm not particularly proud of myself. She sounded really upset. But at least she's coming home now and we can talk about all this.

Damn it. It's a good seven-hour drive from Tenby to here, if not more. Annie's driving back through the rain, tired and upset. What the fuck have I done? If anything happens to her, I'll never forgive myself.

Sunday:
Early hours Sunday morning now. Where the hell is she?

She's here. Thank God.

She's going to be pissed.

Urgh! I hate arguing with Annie. Not only do I feel like I've just kicked a puppy, but she's my best friend. I can't sleep, I'm so wound up.

We shouted at each other until our throats were raw. We've never shouted at each other before. I was angry after we slept together, but as she was crying the next day over what happened, I couldn't bear to shout at her so I just left. Now… everything came out last night and I hate it. I hate what I've become.

It's nearly lunchtime now and I haven't seen Annie since she flounced off to bed last night. She's probably exhausted.

Going for a walk on the beach to clear my head.

I'm so angry at you. I have never been so furious before in my entire life.

My first holiday since Nick died and you ruined it with absurd jealousy, misplaced guilt and anger.

You need to stop feeling guilty over the accident. I don't blame you at all. There was nothing that you could have done and it wasn't your fault. Do you honestly think I wish it was you that had died instead of Nick? I can't believe you said that last night. That thought has never entered my head. I was just so grateful that I hadn't lost both of my best friends that night.

You gave me two million pounds of guilt money? I was so stupid to think that was Nick's insurance money. I still have most of it. I'll arrange for it to be transferred to you tomorrow. I am not taking your pay-offs. I will re-mortgage the house and pay you back the rest. At least then you won't seem to think you have the right to tell me what to do with my life.

As for what happened between us, I don't regret it for one moment. It was not a mistake, well, not for me. I cried the next day because I was so confused by my feelings. Grief is a complicated emotion, as I'm sure you're aware. I cried because I felt no guilt at all for sleeping with you and I felt that I should. Because I bloody well enjoyed it and there was you all angry for letting it happen. I cried because I knew you were going to run, like you always have when times get tough. I cried because I knew you leaving was going to hurt like Nick dying all over again.

Am I supposed to feel like scum because I love you, because I loved you the entire time I was married to Nick? Well I don't. Loving you did not mean that I didn't love Nick. I never settled for Nick. I had the best husband in the world, my best friend. I loved him more every day we were together and there was never a moment that I wished I had married you instead. Nick was perfect for me in every single way. But I still never stopped loving you and Nick knew that. He often joked that we should have joined some weird cult where I could have married you both. That I could have worked out some rota where you both had an equal share of me.

What I do and with who has nothing to do with you. Regardless of the money and that you're Nick's brother, you have no claim over me. How dare you say that I'm being disloyal to Nick by being with these men? It's been two years, do you honestly expect me to be alone for the rest of my life. Do you think that's what Nick would have wanted?

As it happens, nothing happened with Barney or Connor. Connor is gay and camper than Christmas. But Barney was sweet, funny, kind and incredibly patient. When it came down to it, I couldn't do anything with him. I wanted it to be you kissing me and touching me, not him. For some stupid reason I felt like I was being disloyal to you. You, not Nick. How could I be such an idiot when you have so little regard for me?

I want you out of the house and I don't want to see you again.

Annie...

I don't know what to say.

Please, I don't want the money back. I don't need it. I tried to give you guys the money before Nick died and you both were too proud to take it. The one great thing about being a successful writer is being able to look after my family and friends.

We can never be together. Regardless of your opinion of the accident, I know that I should have done something to save my brother. I cannot and will not be the person that kills my brother, then screws his wife.

You're right. I need to leave you to live your own life without interference from me. Can we make a deal? You keep the money and you'll never see me again.

Take care, Annie. I hope you will be happy.

❧

15th to 18th July
Mrs Applecroft

This is not the medium for such discussions. I do not want to read about the sordid sex life of Mrs Butterworth or of any of the other guests that have stayed here. Please keep your private life private and do not air your dirty laundry for all and sundry to see. When I booked this holiday I did not expect to be exposed to this kind of disgusting behaviour.

Quite right, Mrs Applecroft, my apologies.

Wednesday:
I found a pea at the back of the freezer. I would think the freezer would be cleaned out in between guests.

Mrs Butterworth seems to be cultivating weeds in the back garden. There are two big bushes of what are obviously weeds. Admittedly they have purple flowers so it may be hard for the uneducated to identify, but I know a weed when I see one.

The grass out on the green needs cutting.

The sign to Butterworth Farm is <u>still</u> squeaking.

The beach was very cold today.

The carpet in the spare room has an unsightly stain underneath the rug.

The Frog and Rhubarb, which, incidentally, I've always thought was a silly name, charged me two pounds for a portion of chips today. Though the chips tasted good, I will not be going there again and paying those exorbitant prices.

Thursday:
I just came by to drop off some eggs like you asked. I am not responsible for the upkeep of the grass on the green; I suggest you write to the council if it offends you so much.

Nor am I responsible for the squeaky sign to Butterworth Farm or the cold weather.

My apologies for the pea in the freezer, I must have missed it the last time I cleaned it out.

I may be uneducated in the gardening department, but I know what I like and the purple Buddleia is a beautiful plant that encourages butterflies to the garden.

There is nothing I can do about the blackcurrant stain in the spare room. The house is open to children and that is something I will never change. Accidents happen and the only thing that I could do was cover it with a rug. Quite why you are poking around under a rug I don't know.

As for the prices at the Frog and Rhubarb, you will find them more than reasonable when compared with other eating establishments.

I do not appreciate your attitude. I think you'll find that when running a customer-focused business such as this, the customer is always right.

Friday:
The chickens woke me up in the middle of the night squawking and making a terrible racket.

Mrs Butterworth has not brought my eggs as I requested. I have had to have cereal for breakfast.

The chickens were both killed by foxes last night, hence the terrible racket, they obviously won't be bothering you again. But that does go some way to explain why they were not so forthcoming in laying their eggs this morning.

As for the customer always being right, I'm sure we can easily rectify this. After this weekend you will no longer be one of my customers. I am never having you back in this house again. You can take your self-righteousness and stick it up your arse.

Annie, I've just come round to clean after Mrs Applecroft's rather hasty departure. What on earth has got into you? You've been stomping around like a bear with a sore head since Olly left. This is not like you and I'm worried. Mrs Applecroft has been infuriating us both for years and you've never been rude before.

I've just looked back at the messages that you and Olly wrote to each other as you wouldn't tell me what's going on. I had no idea you two slept together, but then I suppose it was none of my business.

You can't leave things like that between you, you've been best friends since you were born. You can't throw away twenty-six years of friendship now. I admit the man is being completely unreasonable, but he's still grieving over Nick. Please talk to him. If you can't be together, then at least you can stay friends. You owe him that.

I don't owe him anything. Apart from two million pounds. The man is an arse.

As for Mrs Applecroft, I'm done with being nice to people who don't deserve it. I invite these people into my home, bend over backwards to make them feel welcome, and when they're rude

I'm just supposed to smile and let them walk all over me? Well, no more. Thanks to the arse, I'm in the fortunate position now where I don't really need the money that these guests provide. If I don't like them, I'll tell them so. I'm not going to be treated like scum anymore, by Olly or by anyone.

Then you're in the wrong line of business. I worked in a hotel for five years before I married Albert. Every morning the guests that were checking out always had some complaint, the beds were too hard, too soft, the water wasn't hot enough or it was too hot. The swimming pool was too small. I had one guest complain that the complimentary champagne we had left in her room tasted like goat's piss. I did point out that it was complimentary and as such wasn't going to be Dom Perignon, but she still insisted on compensation, which we duly gave.
    You are lucky that only Mrs Applecroft has found fault in the cottage so far. Maybe this isn't for you if you can't face customer complaints.

Maybe it isn't. I don't actually want to do this anymore. Being in Wales with Hetty has showed me there's a huge world out there just waiting to be explored. I love the beach here, but there are a million beaches out there that I've yet to see. Life is short, Lord knows we know that, and I want to get out there and see what the world has to offer before the grim reaper sneaks up on me too. My feet are itchy, they have been for years, but I stayed for my dad and Nick. My dad died first, Nick the year after. I stayed here then because of Olly, because this would always be the place he would return home to. But now I have nothing to stay for anymore. Don't get me wrong. I love you like the mum I never had, you will always be special to me. I love William too. I just need to do something for me for a while. The next few weeks are busy with the summer clients, but when it dies down I'm going to look into selling this place.

Damned reverse psychology. I was only saying that because the feisty Annie I know and love would have tried to prove me wrong. I didn't actually mean for you to sell the place and leave Chalk Hill.

Chalk Hill is your home and always will be. And you've worked so hard to establish Willow Cottage as a successful business. Don't throw it away now because of some silly spat with Olly.

It's more than that. I need a fresh start.

✎

25th to 28th July

Imogen Brooke, Charlotte Carlisle, Paige Marsh, Amy Bradley and Sadie Collins.

I'm on my hen weekend with my favourite girlies. We're spending the day at a spa tomorrow, lots of massages and relaxing. We're not doing anything heavy; I'll leave that to the boys. They've gone to Ibiza for the stag do. Dan has insisted that we leave the mobile phones at home, then we won't be tempted to text or phone each other or be wondering why the other person hasn't texted or phoned.

I miss him already.
  Imogen Brooke

Oh for goodness' sake. I'm sure you can spend one weekend away from him; you've got the rest of your lives together. And we may

not be going clubbing or sitting on a beach sipping cocktails, we may be in the back end of nowhere, spending our hen weekend in the dreary inbred capital of Britain, where they shag their cows for entertainment, but we are damned well going to have a good time. We're playing drinking games tonight until one of us pukes and tomorrow we have a few little surprises up our sleeve.
   Amy Bradley

Amy, we did agree: no surprises. And you know I'm not a big drinker.

Well, if you're only going to get drunk once in your life then your hen weekend has to be it. How did you and Dan get together, he likes nothing more than going out and getting drunk.

Leave her alone, Amy. This is her hen weekend and she should be having fun the way she wants to, not the way you want to.
   Paige

Oh shut up, Paige.

Have you two started already? Cut it out, Amy.
   Charlotte

By popular demand we are going to play some drinking games.
   Imogen

Feeling a bit fuzzy now.

I love my girlies, they are the best in the world ever.

Sadie's just been sick.

Amy is singing on the table.

Urgh, think it's definitely time for bed.

Saturday:
We're off to the spa now. I think we're all feeling a little worse for wear this morning. A day being pampered will be just what we need.

I can't believe four weeks today I'll be getting married. Dan and I will be driving straight up here on our wedding night to start the first part of our honeymoon.

That's if the wedding takes place. I've just had a text from Simon, who's on the stag do. It seems Dan is enjoying himself very much.

What does that mean?

Don't be a bitch, Amy.

I'm just saying what everyone else is thinking, Charlotte. You said the same to me last night.

In Dan's defence, he told me the other day how much he really loves Imogen. How he never thought he could love anyone as much as he loved her. So what if he's having fun, he's probably just getting drunk and passing out on the beach. The important thing is that, in four weeks, he will be sliding that ring onto her finger and starting a whole new life together.
  Paige

Can we go to the spa now, instead of writing in this bloody book? I have toes that need a pedicure and a hot stone massage to enjoy.
  Sadie

And Dan said the same to me, that though it was scary committing himself to one woman for the rest of his life, he knew that he would never find anyone that he loved as much as he loved Immy.

Why is it scary?

Spa. NOW!!

Have just got back from a wonderful day at the spa, drinking champagne and being thoroughly pampered. Tonight we're going to watch films and... oh, there's a policeman at the door.

OH MY GOD!! I do so love a man in uniform, even if the uniform didn't stay on for long.

Wahooooooooooooo!!!!!!!!!

As surprises go, this was a damned fine one.
   Charlotte

I don't like strippers; I think they're crass and very embarrassing. However, PC Dick Grandé, as he called himself, was very entertaining. Rubbing baby lotion onto his body was... well, as much as I hate to admit it, this was one fantastic surprise.

Pictures going up on Facebook now!!!
   Amy

Don't you dare! Where's your loyalty? What happens on the hen weekend, stays on the hen weekend.

Keep your hair on.

Sunday:
Just popped by to see if you're all OK. Everyone seems to be in bed, so I'm guessing you've been enjoying yourselves. I saw the police come round last night. Do let me know if you're having any problems or if there's anything I can help you with.
  Annie Butterworth

OK, so just read the last few comments. I realise now that he wasn't a policeman at all, which is something of a relief. We have a non-existent crime rate round here. Apart from the obvious incest and bestiality, Amy!!! Have fun today and don't forget to take the penis ice cube trays home with you. And the six-foot inflatable penis that's flying from the flagpole on the green. And the wind-up swimming penis currently playing with the ducks in the pond. I'm off now to go and shag a cow!!!

Monday:
Thanks, Annie. Sorry about the mess, we cleaned up as much as we could. Sorry about the bestiality and incest comments from Amy too, she was only joking. Will see you in four weeks when I'll be Mrs Edwards!!
  Imogen

⁓

Annie, we need to talk. I know every time we speak lately we just end up arguing about Olly and now you've been studiously avoiding me for the last few days. I don't want to lose you, you mean the world to me. I promise not to talk about him from now on. Whatever you decide to do, I will support you fully.
    We need to talk about something else. I found Nick's will.

I don't think it's a legal document, nothing official, it's a letter that just says on the envelope: 'My Will. Only to be opened in the event of my death'. I was sorting through a cupboard and it fell out of your wedding album. I haven't read it, I thought you should read it first.

What could he possibly leave me, we owned everything equally, he made sure of that.

Maybe, it's just… I don't know, funeral arrangements, which song to play, where he wanted his ashes sprinkled, that sort of thing.

Well, I had him buried, so it better bloody not be. Oh, Sophia! I don't think I want to read it. Not after all this time. I'm finally getting my life back on track and to read it would be taking a step backwards.

Shall I read it, it could be important?

What if it's something I should have done, but didn't? Do I do it now, two years down the line? What if it's something I don't want to do? Do I do it anyway because it's what Nick would have wanted?

I'll leave it here. You can read it if you want.

Oh my god!

What does it say?

Oh my god! I can't believe Nick would do that. No wonder it wasn't written officially, no solicitor in the land would put their name to such conditions. What was he thinking?

I don't know. But I know one thing, Olly is not having 'It'. If Nick was still alive, I'd kill him all over again, how dare he?

You need to tell Olly this. He has a right to know.

No, absolutely not. Then he'll think he has some stupid claim over it. Besides I'm not actually talking to him at the moment.

Don't be a child.

And yes, I know you're sticking your tongue out at me right now.

⚬

1st to 4th August
Mrs Cumblewick

Willow Cottage is a charming little cottage. Thank you so much for letting me bring my pets with me. I would be lost without them. And I know they'd miss their mummy too. Poor Gabriel, the rat, didn't eat the last time I left and Leonard, my parrot, didn't speak to me for a week.

Chalk Hill is so quaint and I love Wells-Next-The-Sea and the cute little beach huts.

Saturday:
I'm going for a walk shortly and will take some of my friends with me. I'm leaving some of them here, so I won't be gone long. Everyone is always so horrible about

Frank and I think it hurts his feelings. People aren't keen on Miranda either, so she can stay here and keep Frank company.

Derek loves the beach and playing in the shallows, I'll just have to watch he doesn't go too deep, tortoises can't swim after all.

Hugo likes it too, though I will have to rub some sun-cream into his bald patches, bless him he's getting old now and losing a lot of his fur. He's lost so much of it that he looks like a piebald goat. I think it's because he gets stroked so much by the little children. They all feel so sorry for him because he's only got three legs.

I'll take Leonard too, though his swearing can be a bit of a problem. I've had some children think I'm a pirate when I wear my big floppy hat and carry Leonard on my shoulder. Then they run over to stroke him and he tells them to fuck off. It doesn't go down well with the parents.

Colin can go in his hamster's ball, though he and Stan don't get on well. The last time we came to the beach, Stan rolled him down the seafront and then buried him in the sand. I've told Colin that it's not Stan's fault. With only one good eye, the poor dog gets confused sometimes and thinks Colin's ball is a real one, I don't think Stan sees that Colin is inside. Colin doesn't believe it though. Last time I let him run round the lounge, he snuck up on Stan and bit him on the tail. The howling sent poor Leonard into a right tizz. He was swearing about it for days.

Just got back from our walk. Leonard was on his best behaviour and only swore once. It was a shame it was the C word and that he used it when a policeman was walking past. I managed to keep Stan away from Colin.

Unfortunately, a cricket ball landed on Derek and cracked his shell so I've just Sellotaped it back up with brown parcel tape.

Oh dear, just realised that Miranda's vivarium is empty. She hasn't eaten since Tuesday, so she'll be hungry.

I can't find Gabriel either. He doesn't like the sand getting in his whiskers so I left him in my knitting basket, but now he's not there. I've told Miranda not to eat the others and how angry I was that she ate Eric last year. Being eaten is no way to go.

I've searched everywhere for Miranda. She's a big python too; I thought I would have found her by now.

Screams coming from next door. That normally is a good indicator of Miranda's presence. I don't know why people scream when they see her. It's not like she's big enough to eat a human.

Just hurried next door to find Annie's friend, Sophia, standing on a chair screaming and Annie picking up Miranda and telling her how beautiful she was.

I felt very proud of Miranda, she is one of the most beautiful snakes I've ever seen and not many people tell her so. I was quite pleased by Annie's reaction to Miranda and how kind she was to her, but Annie went down in my estimations with her reaction to Frank. As Annie was helping me put Miranda back in her vivarium, she noticed Frank in his tank and freaked out. She got quite fussy about him, saying that he'd better not escape and end up next door or he'd end up being a flat tarantula. I don't know why people are so horrid. It must upset him to hear such things.

It does seem though that Gabriel has been eaten, Miranda has a suspicious bulge in her stomach which looks to be rat-sized. I've told her off and she looks very apologetic, but poor Gabriel, he was so looking forward to coming on holiday as well.

Mrs Cumblewick, I'm so sorry to hear about Gabriel's death. We get so attached to our pets. My chickens were killed by foxes recently and I was so upset.

When we spoke on the phone and you asked if you could bring your pets, I had no idea you meant a dog, a goat, a hamster, a rat, a snake, a tarantula and a parrot. Oh and a goldfish, I just spotted him on top of the TV. Oh and a tortoise too, I didn't notice him because he was covered in parcel tape.

I'm sorry I wasn't kind about Frank; I do have a bit of a spider phobia. It doesn't make sense, we are so much bigger than them, but then phobias aren't rational. Some people are scared of heights, or closed spaces, some people even have a phobia of beards or cheese. I think being scared of something with eight hairy legs and fangs makes more sense than being scared of a block of cheese from Asda.

Could I ask that you tether your goat in the garden so he can't reach the plants in the borders? I want Hugo to enjoy his holiday too, but I see that he has taken a liking to some of the flowers already and I would like my garden to be enjoyed by future guests. Could you also keep an eye on Derek for the same reasons? And it might be an idea to keep your pets indoors at night. As I said, we have a lot of foxes around here and I would hate for any more of your beloved pets to meet the same fate as my chickens or poor Gabriel.

Annie Butterworth

I understand your phobia, not everyone can be as level-headed as me. I do have a terrible phobia of cling film, but I think that's quite a rational fear.

I appreciate your kindness over allowing my pets to stay, not many hotels or holiday cottages are as patient or kind. I will do my best to ensure Derek and Hugo don't eat all your lovely flowers. I've told them not to and normally they are quite obedient.

As for the foxes, none of my animals will be outside after dark. Apart from Miranda, Frank, Leonard and Goldie, all the other animals will be sleeping in the bed with me. Don't worry, they're all perfectly house-trained.

Strange. Annie has just read my message and walked away laughing to herself. Not quite sure what's so funny.

Sunday:
Another lovely day at the beach today with my pets. I feel like the pied piper sometimes with the children that hang around, stroking and playing with all the animals.

Have just lit a fire as Hugo and Stan love curling up in front of it. Poor Derek is having a really rough weekend. Somehow he got too close to the flames and the parcel tape caught fire. I only just managed to put it out in time before it spread. Now his shell is looking a bit black and singed. Leonard keeps laughing at him and telling him he's an idiot.

Monday:
Had a lovely weekend and all the animals had a great

time too. Well, apart from Derek and poor Gabriel. We'll come again soon.

We'd be glad to have you back any time.

Annie, are you mad? I would think that now Mrs Cumblewick has left, you'd be slamming the proverbial stable door and never having her back again. You moan about Mrs Applecroft being rude, but you open your arms to the entire freaky menagerie of Mrs Cumblewick?

Well, once I'd got over the shock of seeing a tarantula in Willow Cottage, I was OK with it. Admittedly, a woman who sleeps in the same bed as a three-legged goat, a half-blind dog, a hamster and a tortoise with a cracked shell is clearly madder than a box of frogs, but as she quite rightly pointed out, they were all house-trained.

In some ways animals are easier to deal with than rude customers. Apart from their fondness for eating each other, they generally seem to be quite civil.

Apart from Leonard. It seems poor David Lambeth was the policeman that Leonard swore at down at the beach the other day. I think David was quite embarrassed.

Ah, a foul-mouthed parrot is the least of my worries. I'd rather that than rude customers.

It's nice to see the smile back on your face again after all the stress with Olly over the last few weeks. I know we haven't spoken about it for a while, but have you had any more thoughts about the will?

Yes. I'm not doing anything about it and I expect you to keep your promise and not tell Olly either. Nick had no right to leave it to Olly in the will and after Olly's attitude the last time he was here, he certainly isn't having it.

Have you spoken to him at all?

No.

Have you?

A bit. He's miserable.

Of his own making.

I know.

Damn it, I don't want him to be miserable.

Tell him about the will, please.

No, absolutely not.

&

8th to 11th August
Gladys Clearwater and Madge Ambrose

Friday:
We are here for the Eastern regional championships of the Great Cake Baking Challenge. We have left the men at home to fend for themselves and we have come to represent the town of Beccles.

90

The regional championships take place every year in the town of the previous year's winner. Last year's winner, a Sophia Lorenzo, comes from this neck of the woods and so we find ourselves here.

Of course we won our town's qualifying round and the Suffolk County Championships and now we are here, ready to take part in the regional championships.

Gladys

MAY I just REMINd you THAT WE GOT THIS FAR LAST YEAR, oNly TO bE pipped TO THE post AT THE LAST sECONd.

MAdGE

Yes, but this year we have the secret ingredient.

Gladys!! WE ARE usiNG colA; THERE is NOTHING uNusuAl AbOUT THAT.

Of course not.

I've just been reading back over some of the comments in this book. It seems we have entered the camp of the enemy. Sophia Lorenzo is a cleaner here and a very good friend of the landlady, Annie Butterworth. We will have to watch our backs.

Hi ladies.
Just popped by to see how you're settling in. I hope you do really well in the competition on Sunday. I know Sophia is looking forward to it too. I'm sure you're only joking about 'the enemy's

camp'. There are no enemies here, just lots of fantastic cooks taking part in a friendly cake competition. If you want me to trial any of your cakes tomorrow, I'd be more than happy to be the guinea pig.

Mmm, so you can steal all our ideas? I don't think so!

Madge, Annie is right. Of course Sophia is not our mortal enemy. We'd be happy to let you have a try of our competition entry tomorrow if there's any going spare.

We have a big day tomorrow, refining our entry for Sunday, so we're off to bed now.

Saturday:
We've done this recipe so many times, we could do it in our sleep. We're just going for a walk to clear our heads and talk tactics before we make the final piece.

Ladies, Annie told me you were entering in the regional finals tomorrow. Just popped by to wish you both luck. I've had cola cakes in the past, but I've never had one I've enjoyed before. I'm sure yours will be different though. Of course I didn't win the national championships last year, but I did come second and I got a free night at the Hilton in London. It would be lovely to see you at the nationals this year, it's a shame only one of us can win at the regionals tomorrow.
    Good luck. Sophia

Cow.

Madge!!

We have just finished making two cakes from the same batch. We will trial one and, if it's not good enough, we have time to make a second batch.

I've been called over to test the apple and cola cake. It smells delicious and I can't wait to try it.

Oh, the cake tastes fantastic, it's so yummy.

Just had my second slice and the ladies are so lovely to talk to. They make me laugh a lot.

Third slice before I go. It's so moreish.

We are off out for another walk now, but it seems we have done well.

I've just snuck back in. I can't get enough of this cake. It's soooo good.

The sky is so blue, like the sea on a hot summer's day. The clouds are all fluffy like candy floss. I've never noticed before just how green the leaves are outside. I feel like writing a poem about them.

The Green Leaves of Wells
Chime in the wind like bells.

OK, I've never been good at poetry before but that is pure brilliance.

Just one more slice of cake, then I must go and see William and the cows.

I've just phoned Olly, he didn't answer so I spoke to his answer-phone. I told him I loved him and wanted lots of his babies. He's going to be so mad when he gets that message. I can't stop laughing about it.

I've just phoned him again and told him he was a pompous git and that he needed to remove his head from his rather gorgeous arse and see the bigger picture. I think he might be mad about that too.

I've just been wandering around Willow Cottage. It feels quite naughty, as if I'm snooping around someone else's home even though it's mine. It really is a lovely cottage; Nick would have been so pleased with what I have done with it.

Oh my god! There is a hole in the downstairs bathroom, it's only small but if you lie down on the floor you can see right through to my bathroom next door. You can see the whole of the shower and the sink and the toilet. Thankfully I don't use that bathroom very often, as I have a rather posh en-suite upstairs. Must remember to seal it up so I don't have any peeping toms.

Olly just phoned me back. He accused me of being drunk. Cheeky sod, it's only two o'clock in the afternoon. I told him he was a rude and arrogant arse. I also told him he wasn't having it no matter what Nick says. Though Olly didn't know what 'IT' was that he wasn't having. I told him it was mine and he wouldn't have it, even if he begged for it. I read him some of my rather brilliant poetry and then he got all stern and asked what I had been taking. After that I hung up. He phoned me back twice but I didn't answer. He's going to be properly mad. It's so funny.

Sophia has just phoned me too to ask if I'm drunk. She is somewhere else today. She did say when I saw her this morning. But, for the life of me, I can't remember. Olly has obviously rung her to get her to check on me. Stupid arse. Why on earth would I be drunk? I feel great.

I do feel tired actually. I might go for a kip. Just one more slice before I go to bed.

Oh dear. Luckily the judges will only be having one slice tomorrow.

It does seem that the cake is quite addictive. Who would have thought our little old apple and cola cake would have such an effect?

Sunday:
The day of the competition. Our wonderful cake will soon wipe the smile off Sophia Lorenzo's face.

We have to be there shortly, so we'd better pack up our cake and head down there.

Oh god! Woke up this morning with a banging headache after passing out seemingly for over nineteen hours. Have just thrown up as if it was an Olympic event. I can only assume there was something dodgy about that cake. After eating it, the afternoon passed in a blurry haze. I've just rushed round to tell the ladies that I had some severe kind of food poisoning from it so they don't take it to the cake competition, but they've already left.

Crap! Just read my messages from yesterday, which I have no recollection of writing. I phoned Olly? I don't even remember doing that, let alone what I said. Though from my previous messages, it clearly wasn't good. Where the hell is my mobile phone? I need to apologise to him.

Have just found it in the fridge! Twelve answerphone messages and eleven very rude ones from Olly, so there's no way I'm apologising now. One concerned message from Sophia. I have a vague recollection of her checking on me last night.

I need to get down to the cake competition to stop the judges and other competitors from getting food poisoning like I did.

Monday:
Just here to clean Willow Cottage after the fiasco that was the cake competition yesterday.

Gladys and Madge entered their apple and Cola cake, which was tested by a panel of three judges. They loved it and decreed them the winner. The other competitors also tasted it and loved it. I, thankfully, declined to try it.

Unfortunately one bite was seemingly not enough and by the time Annie turned up, there was a crowd of people around the cake like flies round shit, jostling and pushing each other so they could have a second, third and fourth slice. Soon a fight broke out. Eleanor McGrew, one of the judges, ended up with a broken nose. Kevin Peterson got a black eye. The police had to break it up. When they realised that the fight was over the cake, they knew something was suspicious.

With Annie's version of events added to the mix, it was quite obvious that they were dealing with cannabis or something similar.

Gladys and Madge were arrested for possession of drugs. They were bailed and have just returned, rather shame-faced, to the cottage to collect their things. As there was no cake left, there is no hard evidence against them and it's likely that the charges will be dropped.

What's worse was that the judging panel obviously disqualified their cake from the competition, but were too stoned or beaten up to be able to declare a new winner, which would obviously have been mine. It's a shambles!

There is going to be a new Eastern Regional Championship later on in the year. Thankfully, Gladys and Madge will not be allowed to enter.

And you thought I was drunk! Cheek!

To be fair, anyone talking to you yesterday would have thought that, you were giggly and saying all sorts of silly things. I have phoned Olly to explain the reason behind your madness. I believe he has phoned you to apologise?

You should have heard the rude messages that he left for me on Saturday. He can stick his apology up his arse.

You did tell him you loved him and wanted lots of his babies.

Unfortunately, that part is true.

Oh, Annie!

I also told him he's never having it, and I stand by that.

And, yes, I'm well aware you're rolling your eyes at me right now.

❧

16th to 23rd August
The Meechams And Max

We have a new dog called Max. He is a Cock Spanul and has big flappy curly ears. We are going to take him to the beach later. It will be his first time he has seen the sea. I think he is very excited.

Megan Aged 7

Erm, Cocker Spaniel.
  Ben Meecham, Aged 37 ½

Daddy, adults don't put their ages after their names, only children do.

Sorry, Pickle.

Sunday:
Max loved the beach yesterday. He kept running out into the sea and then running back in when the waves came in and barking at them. He dug big holes in the sand and sprayed sand all over our ice cream. Isabelle put her ice cream in Max's fur but Daddy just took Max into the sea to wash him and when he came back he shook water all over us and then Daddy did the same.

Today we went for a walk around the rivers and Max jumped in and got all muddy then he jumped up at Mummy and got muddy paw prints on her jeans. Mummy didn't mind, but Daddy said Max would have to have lessons when we go back home. I wonder how good he is at maths. Mrs Dunston my teacher says I am very good at maths. I can do sums like $45 + 45 = 90$ and I know that it equals 90 very fast. My Aunty Holly says I have big brains. But my brain can't be bigger than the other children because then I would have a big head. Did you know that the Egjiptians thought brains were useless and let the cats eat them but other organs they put in jars like big jam jars called canopic jars. We made one at school and mine had a dog head on it like Max. Dogs are called jackals in Egjipt.

Monday:
Max ran next door today as the gate between our garden and Annie's garden was left open and he put muddy paw prints up her windows. I thought she might shout at Max when she came out but she was stroking him all over and he was wagging his tail so hard that his hole body was wagging. Daddy said he was very sorry and he said that he would clean the windows and when he did he kept looking for Mr Butterworth who we met last time but Annie said that he wasn't here and Daddy was really dissappointed. I'm very dissappointed too. Mr Butterworth is a writer and I wanted to show him my story. He said he would read it the last time I was here and I brought it up here specially.

Tuesday:
I hope you're all settled in. Megan, if you want to give me your story I can fax it over to Olly, Mr Butterworth, for him to see.

Just been next door with Annie. She took my story and posted it through a machine. It came out the other end. She said the machine had taken a photo of my story and sent the photo to Mr Butterworth's fax machine. Annie said his fax machine would then print it out exactly the same as my story and even with all the pictures. Annie also wrote a note to send to Mr Butterworth too. She said the story was from his youngest fan. When I asked what a fan was she said Daddy was a fan of Mr Butterworth because he liked his books. I've seen Mr Butterworth's books. One had a picture of something weird on the front. It was a door with red paint coming out from underneath. Daddy said it was red paint but then Mummy gave him that look she gives him when he is telling lies. I wonder why Mr Butterworth is not here. Mummy said that Mr Butterworth wasn't really Annie's husband but he was her husband's brother which is why they have the same last name. Mummy said that her husband had died and that her husband's brother Oliver had lied about him being her husband because sometimes it is easier to lie to children than explain the truth. I said that Mr Butterworth the one that is still alive should marry Annie and Mummy said that it doesn't work like that because when you get married both people need to love each other very much. But last time we were here Mr Butterworth, the alive one, kept giving Annie looks the same looks that Daddy gives Mummy that shows that Daddy loves Mummy more than chocolate. Daddy loves chocolate very much.

Wednesday:
I was going to bed last night and Mummy was reading me a story and Max was snoring on my pillow and Annie came round. I heard her talking to Daddy downstairs and after she left Daddy came up and he was very excited and he had a piece of paper that had come from the fax machine. Mr Butterworth had sent me a message saying he loved my story and specially loved the pictures. He liked the part about the dragon the best and said that I should keep writing stories all the time and I would get better and better and better at it. He told Annie to give me the mug he had painted at her shop, it said World's Best Writer on the side. I am so happy he liked my story. I'm going to show my teacher his letter

when I go back to school because she is a fan of Mr Butterworth's too. I heard her say to Miss Kane that he is fit and Miss Kane said she wouldn't say no. I asked Mummy what she wouldn't say no to and Mummy just said that Miss Kane liked his books too and then Daddy gave her one of the looks he gives her when she is lying. I wonder why adults lie so much. Daddy says it is wrong to lie.

We had another day at the beach today and Max chased the seagulls. Isabelle was watching him and couldn't stop laughing. Her giggerling was very funny and Mummy and Daddy were laughing at her. Then a big seagull chased Max away from a sandwitch and Max was scared and came back to us but then he found a ball and ran away with it. There was a family there whose ball it was and they thought it was funny that Max was stealing it. The boys were chasing Max down the beach and Max thought it was all a game.

Thursday:
Max has got a sore paw from something on the beach. He keeps hopping around and crying. Annie said there was a new man that had moved into the village that was a vet and she would get him to come over and look at Max. His name was Barney and he was very friendly to Max and to me. But then Mummy came in and she knew Barney. She went very red and Barney went red and Daddy wanted to know why they were both red and Mummy said that she used to go out with Barney years and years and years ago before she met Daddy. Daddy shook Barney's hand very hard and said it was nice to meet him but he had that look on his face that said he was lying about it being nice to meet him. Barney took something sharp out of Max's paw and told Mommy that she would have to clean it regularrly so it didn't get in fected.

We're going to the beach now but Daddy is staying at home with Max. Daddy said it would be best not to take Max to the beach today so his paw can get better but Mummy said Daddy was being silly and that it was years and years ago. But Max only hurt his paw yesterday.

When we came back from the beach we bumped into Barney again and Mummy and Barney was talking and Barney said he thought about her sometimes and that he was happy that she was happy and Mummy said she was very happy and that Daddy makes her happy and the girls made her happy. I think she was talking about me and Isabelle and Barney said that was good and then he hugged her and she hugged him and when we went back to the house Daddy was watching us from the window. Daddy cooked us toad in the hole which is my favourite. When we were eating dinner Mummy and Daddy didn't talk and it was very quiet and I didn't like it. Daddy talked to me about the beach but they didn't talk to each other. Max was begging for food and Mummy gave him a bit of her sausage. Then Daddy told her off about feeding Max from the table and she said that she didn't want it. Daddy said that maybe his sausage wasn't good enough for her and maybe she would prefer Barney's sausage instead. Then Mummy got up from the table and said Daddy was being ridickulous.

Saturday:
When I went into Mummy and Daddy's room this morning Mummy was sitting on Daddy's lap and they were kissing and both naked. Then Daddy kissed Mummy's boobs which made me laugh and Mummy went all red again when she saw me. Daddy was laughing. Mummy told me to clean my teeth and go downstairs and that they would be down in a minute to make pancakes for breakfast. I like pancakes. It's

my favourite breakfast ever. I've cleaned my teeth really quickly and I'm playing with Max downstairs while they get dressed. I think they are jumping up and down on the bed like a trampoline because the bed is squeaking. Daddy says I shouldn't jump up and down on the bed because I might break it. It's funny that adults can do things that children are not allowed to do.

Just had pancakes and we are going down the beach again before we leave. Mummy and Daddy were kissing a lot in the kitchen when Mummy was washing up and Daddy was giving her his look, the same look he gives chocolate cake. Mummy was looking at him like he was ice cream. Mummy loves ice cream.

Oh God!!! Out of the mouths of babes.

Oh my god!! I forget how astute she is getting now.

$\sim$

23rd to 30th August
~~*Imogen and Dan Edwards*~~
Imogen Brooke

Thanks for the champagne, Annie; I shall enjoy drinking that on my own later.

Dan The Bastard Edwards didn't bother to show for our wedding. What was worse was he didn't even have the decency to let me know. I was standing there, my brides-maids, my flower girls, the groomsmen, his best man, his

103

parents, my parents, hell my entire family, my work colleagues, everyone was there waiting for him to turn up. And he never did. We waited, we waited some more. I phoned him, Simon his best man phoned him, we all phoned him. Eventually his brother got hold of him, and he said three words before he hung up: 'I'm not coming'. 'I'm not coming'!? No why or how, just 'I'm not coming'.

Amy Bradley, an old friend of Dan's and someone I've never liked but tried to welcome into my social group, had the audacity to say: 'I told you so.' So I punched her in the face and left.

I can't bear to see all those sympathetic faces, 'Poor Imogen, jilted at the altar', 'Such a lovely girl, so sweet, so nice, how could anyone do this to her?'

Well fuck being nice, fuck you all. I'm going to enjoy this honeymoon without Dan The Bastard and on Saturday I'll fly to Venice on my own.

Sunday:
I'm so sorry to hear this. Though sympathy is not what you want right now, I get that.
    Annie Butterworth

How would you have any fucking idea what I want right now, with your beautiful, cute cottage with roses growing up the fucking door, your beautiful, perfect garden and your beautiful, perfect fucking husband who probably fucks you every night in your great big fucking four-poster bed. You have no idea what I am going through right now. Dan was supposed to be my happy ever after.

You're right, I have no idea what it's like to be jilted at the altar. But I do have some idea what it's like to be on the receiving end of those sympathetic looks and how desperately

104

you want to get away from them. I do have some idea what that heart-breaking feeling is like when you're completely in love with someone and you lose that person for ever or to not have those feelings returned in the first place.

Your husband fucked you over as well, did he?

My husband died, which pissed me off no end. The day after we put him in the ground, I went down to the graveyard and shouted at his gravestone for a full hour. Then I smashed a vase of flowers on his grave and told him he didn't deserve to have fucking flowers because he shouldn't have left me.

He used to love walking and someone bought him a hiking stick which he used once. I told him he looked like an idiot walking around with it, and after that he'd carry it on every walk we went on, just to annoy me. Well, that was propped up against the gravestone and I grabbed that and started beating the gravestone with it. The stick got ruined, the flowers got squashed, the police got called and I didn't give a shit. Until a few days later, when the grief finally caught up with me and I didn't stop crying for months. I've had nothing but sympathetic looks for the last two years. So I do have some idea what you are going through right now. Some.

I couldn't help giggling at the idea of you standing over a gravestone beating it to death with a hiking stick. Sorry.

Yes, looking back I must have looked like a madwoman. The elderly vicar who tried to stop me desecrating Nick's grave has never looked at me the same way since. I think he thought I was possessed by the devil when I growled at him to fuck off or I'd rip his fucking head off. He ran back inside the church so quickly, then came out a few minutes later and threw holy water all over me. You can imagine how well that went down. I started *chasing him round the graveyard with the hiking stick. He was screaming for help, screaming that I was going to kill him. I might have done as well if I had caught him, but he was quite sprightly for someone so old and managed to get away.*

Sorry, I know I shouldn't laugh but you do paint quite a picture.

It's fine. Grief and anger will do strange things to you. It's OK to grieve over what has happened, just don't do anything stupid you'll regret later. And if you need to talk or get drunk with someone, I'm only next door.

Thanks.

Monday:
Feeling a bit better today. Still upset, still angry, but less likely to rip someone's head off or chase them round a graveyard with a hiking stick. If Dan had showed up on Saturday night or even yesterday, I think it highly likely I would have killed him. And not metaphorically or figuratively, but literally. I feel a bit calmer now. The beach does seem to have that effect on me. My apologies, Annie, if anything I said or wrote upset you.

My phone has been ringing nonstop since I ran out of my wedding on Saturday. No one knows where I am and I guess the last place they would look would be our honeymoon cottage. I've texted my mum to say I'm fine but just need some time to think. Word must have filtered through to my friends as the phone calls have stopped and I'm now just getting supportive texts instead. Nothing from Dan The Bastard.

I don't think I'd kill him now, if I saw him, though I'm

still seriously considering cutting off his balls and forcing him to eat them.

Just dropping off a lasagne in case you don't feel like cooking. You probably don't feel like eating either.

Thanks, Annie.

Tuesday:
Going out for another walk on the beach. I feel even calmer today.

Hi, Immy. Annie let me in, reluctantly.

I'm so very sorry for what happened on Saturday. I panicked. I love you so much. There has never been any woman before you that I've loved half as much as I love you and there never will be.

I don't want to put the blame on anyone else; I know I have to take full responsibility myself. However, the boys have been winding me up ever since I proposed about what I would be giving up, how I wouldn't be allowed out with them anymore, how I'd have to stay in with you every night. On the stag do, I just started to think how much I would miss them, miss the antics we get up to.

Amy kept saying that tying myself to one woman would be a mistake, that I would get bored and start to resent you. I didn't want to resent you. She started saying that after the wedding, children would come next, there'd be sleepless nights and dirty nappies and screaming kids and I definitely wouldn't be allowed out to play then and I wasn't sure if I was ready for all that.

This is so hard. I wish you were here and I could wrap my arms around you and tell you how I feel. Though after reading the previous comments you have written in this book, maybe for my safety, it's best that you aren't here.

I love you. I can't live my life without you. I want to be with you and embrace all that that entails. If you take me back, I promise never to hurt you ever again.

I will be in The Frog and Rhubarb, across the green, if you want to talk.

I hope you want to talk.
  Dan The Bastard

Oh!

I have asked Dan back here as I didn't want to conduct our affairs in public, but now I don't know what to say. He keeps trying to hold me, to talk to me, but I don't want him anywhere near me. He's apologised a thousand times but it's not enough. I don't know what I want from him anymore. How can we just go back to how we were?

We have spent the last two hours at opposite ends of the lounge, deliberately avoiding eye contact. The silence is unbearable.

I have asked Annie to make up the bed in the spare room. I can't sleep next to him tonight as if everything was all right between us. To Annie's credit she has done this without a single word. I thought she might wade in with her penny's worth or glare at Dan or say something sympa-

thetic to me, but she acted as if making the spare bedroom
up for a couple was the most normal thing in the world.

Are we still a couple?

Do we have any future at all?

Going to bed now, I feel exhausted. Maybe things will
look brighter tomorrow. Maybe.

Wednesday:
Clearly you feel you can communicate easier through
this book than directly with me at the moment. I don't
blame you; I wouldn't want to talk to me either. But if
this is the only way you will talk to me then fine.

Everything moved so quickly. I never wanted to get
married, it wasn't on my radar at all. I was one of the
lads, out almost every night of the week, getting drunk,
getting laid. You know my past; I've been completely
honest with you there. Then you came along and
everything changed. There hasn't been another woman
since you, not on the stag do, never. I've not so much as
kissed another woman since I met you. I never even
wanted to. No one ever came close.
 I wanted to spend every single second with you; I
didn't want to be with the lads anymore. Of course, every
time I cancelled plans with them they'd take the piss.
'Under the thumb', they said, 'Staying at home with the
ball and chain'. At first, I just laughed it off but then it
started to get annoying.
 Then, one drunken New Year's Eve, I looked into your
eyes and knew I wanted to spend every single New Year's
Eve with you, that life wouldn't be the same without you

and I proposed. I've never regretted it. The next day, I walked around with a huge grin on my face, but then the jibes started.

And shortly after that, my lovely, sweet, beautiful girlfriend disappeared and Bridezilla appeared. Everything, I mean everything, was about the wedding. The perfect flowers, the perfect dress, the photographer, the videographer, the five-tiered cake, the shoes, the arrival music, the walking down the aisle music, the signing the certificate music, the DJ versus a live band dilemma, the food, the canapés, the drinks, the hotel, the church, the cars, the best man, the groomsmen, the nightmare that was the choice of bridesmaids, the flower girls, the page boys, what your mum was going to wear, what my mum was going to wear, the colour scheme, the favours, the invites, the confetti, the honeymoon, the guests and who to invite. I felt like I was drowning. I have had this huge sense of claustrophobia for the last six months. We have spent every single weekend at wedding fairs collating ideas, every single night talking about all of the above. It has been all-consuming from the day after New Year's Day; we haven't talked about anything else since.

I lost sight of the reason why I wanted to marry you, all I could see was weddings, weddings, weddings and could no longer see our beautiful future together. You wanted us to write our own vows. I'm rubbish at all that, the fear of being the centre of attention anyway was scary, but coming up with a speech, to declare my love for you in my own words, was terrifying. What if it sounded crap, what if it didn't do my feelings justice? You wrote your vows so easily and, night after night, I stared at a sheet of blank paper willing the inspiration to come to me and it never did. Amy said if I couldn't

*come up with the words to tell you I loved you, maybe I
really didn't, or maybe I didn't love you enough. I know
I shouldn't have listened to her, but with the stress of
the wedding, with the never-ending jibes from the lads,
I couldn't help letting it all get to me.*

*I realise now what an idiot I have been. That I love
you so much and I want to be with you, for ever. I know
that I hurt you, but if you let me, I will spend every day
for the rest of our lives trying to prove to you how much
I love you.*

I wanted it all to be perfect, because that was the first
day of our perfect life together. You were going to be
my Happy Ever After and I wanted the perfect day to
celebrate that. I'm sorry that I got so caught up in it all,
but you should have talked to me, you should have told
me how you felt.

And can't you see what Amy was trying to do, from the
word go she was trying to break us apart. Your so-called
friend and she was out to ruin everything.

*I don't think she was trying to break us up, I think she
was just concerned that I was doing the wrong thing.*

She clearly wanted you for herself.

*We have never had that relationship. I don't see her that
way, she knows that.*

Doesn't stop her trying to split us up though.

*Maybe. I'll never see her again if that's what you want.
You're the only one that matters now.*

111

Have I ever tried to stop you seeing your mates, Amy included? Do you think I ever would? You shouldn't have paid any attention to her, to any of them. If they were any kind of friends they would have understood that things change, they would have been happy for you.

I've spoken a lot to my friends over the last few days. Every single one of them, well, except Amy, has told me what a fool I was (the words they chose were much ruder than that), that you were the best thing that ever happened to me and I was an absolute shit for standing you up. They said that the jibes, the taking the piss, was just that, just jokes, and I should never have taken it seriously.

So because your friends have backed down, you've changed your mind about not being with me. You should have been strong enough to stand up to them in the first place. Maybe Amy was right, maybe you don't love me enough. If you loved me enough, you would have turned up on Saturday, you would have wanted to be with me regardless. You would have seen past the neurotic bridezilla and seen the person you fell in love with, the person that you asked to marry, the person you were supposed to spend the rest of your life with. How could everything we shared, all those years, mean nothing to you?

I love you, I'm here now. Does that mean nothing to you? I made a mistake, I'm sorry. If we got married we would have had rows, would you have run at the first hurdle or would you have forgiven me and moved on?

I guess we'll never know.

Thursday:
Immy has barely said a single word to me since I've arrived. Though she did offer me a cup of tea this morning at breakfast which I took to be a good sign.

It was tea, simple as that.

What do you want from me, Immy?

What are you offering?

Whatever you want, whatever it takes to get you back.

A big wedding, five hundred guests, you stand up in the church and say loudly and clearly your own vows to prove how much you love me.

Fine. I'll do anything.

I don't really want all that. Maybe I lost my way a bit too. Maybe I got caught up in the moment and forgot what our wedding should have been about. All it should have been was me and you declaring our love for each other and promising to love each other for as long as we both shall live. We didn't need all the frills.

I was happy to give you the frills; I wanted you to be happy.

I know. Then it consumed me. I'm sorry.

Don't apologise. Please don't apologise.

I want kids, loads of them.

I want kids too. I want to start a family with you. I want to be a grown-up now.

I fell in love with the happy, fun Dan. I don't want that to change.

I'm going for a walk on the beach. I'm not saying I'll talk to you or hold your hand, but maybe you could come with me.

I'd like that.

Hi, just popped by to check you hadn't killed each other.

Not that I'm meddling at all, well maybe a little bit, but there is a registry office about five minutes from here. Just saying...

It started with a kiss. Three years ago, that was how it all started. Today it seems we have started all over again.

I'm not waiting three years to marry you again.

What are you suggesting?

That Annie might have a point.

You still want to marry me?

I love you. You being an idiot hasn't changed that.

Friday:
Oh God! Why is making up soooo good?

114

Imogen!! What happened to the sweet, lovely girl I fell in love with?

She's still here, but she's a little bit harder round the edges now.

I think I love 'hard around the edges' Imogen that little bit more. Especially if last night was anything to go by. Bloody hell!!

Dan!!!! You do make me laugh.

Marry me, Imogen. Marry me today and let's go to Venice tomorrow as husband and wife.

We can't just get married today.

Why not? I believe you have the dress.

What about our friends, our family?

It's not about them, it's about us.

If you want to wait, if you want to do it all properly again at the big hotel with the five-tiered cake, we will, I will do whatever it takes to make you happy. But I just want to be married to you now. I want you as my wife.

Your mum won't be happy.

I don't care.

Saturday:
I can't stop grinning.

Yesterday we grabbed Annie and a lady called Sophia and ran down to the registry office. It's not as romantic as you see in the movies where the couple decide to get married on the spur of the moment. Apparently you have to register the wedding weeks in advance just in case anyone wants to object. However we had already done this with the church where we were supposed to marry last week. Although it was unorthodox, the registry office contacted the church and, after a long chat, the registry office decided to marry us.

It was short, but what mattered was we promised to love each other as long as we both shall live. And that was all I needed, I didn't need the all-singing, all-dancing wedding with all the frills, I didn't need Dan to write his own vows, I just needed him standing next to me, holding my hand.

We are now married. I am Mrs Edwards.

We're flying off to Venice today for the second part of our honeymoon. Dan can't stop smiling either.

Thanks, Annie xx

❧

30th August to 4th September
Daisy and Eric Brownlow

The sun is shining, the sea breeze is mild. The conditions couldn't be better for our week's holiday.

Eric and I are naturists and as Holkham Beach, just down the road from here, is an official naturist beach, we are going to give it a try.

There are lots of naturist beaches around the UK that we have visited over the years, some good, some bad and some ugly. Holkham Beach has a good reputation; it has the dunes for added privacy and protection from the wind.

There is nothing more exhilarating or liberating than walking over the hills or beaches without clothes. The feel of the wind on your skin is wonderful.

Daisy Brownlow

Sunday:

We spent a lovely day at the beach yesterday. There were quite a few other naturists, probably over a hundred, who were also enjoying the sun.

Mostly the Textiles did mix amicably with the naturists, most of them are aware that we have a beach for nudists here. Though you always get the poor, unsuspecting tourists that don't see or read the signs and then get the shock of their lives to see us lot romping around in our birthday suits.

The wind did get up a bit and we retreated into the dunes to have our picnic.

We intend to enjoy the beautiful garden here at Willow Cottage today. It is secluded and protected by high trees.

We have nothing to hide or be embarrassed by, but sometimes people get offended by naturists. Annie's cottage does overlook our garden though. So I have been round to see Annie to ask if she would be offended by our nudity and she said it was fine.

Why would she be offended? There is nothing wrong with the naked body. It's perfectly natural. Besides, I imagine she's been running this place for years, she's seen it all.

Eric

Have just skimmed back through this book. A couple of weeks ago she had a woman who brought her snake and a three-legged goat. Now if that doesn't say freak to you, I don't know what does. We are not freaks.

Monday:

We went for a walk over the hills today. Mostly we wait until we are away from the roads before we disrobe. Some people can get funny about it.

Most of the walkers we passed had the typical reaction; shock, amusement and embarrassment, but towards the end we had an unfortunate encounter with a young family. The mother shielded the kids' eyes as we walked towards them and shouted at us that we should be ashamed of ourselves.

Eric is eighty-two and I'm eighty-one, there is very little that causes us to be ashamed at our time of life. Life is too short to have regrets or to live it as others see fit. Of course we covered ourselves up temporarily until they passed. That's generally the naked walker's unwritten code. If it upsets someone then cover up.

What concerns me is that those children will grow up thinking that nudity is something to be ashamed about, that it's disgusting and depraved. There is nothing more natural than being naked. We should be proud of our bodies, not hide them away just because of social conventions. Children are naturally curious when seeing naked people and, with the right parenting, you can explain that naturism is just a personal choice.

Tuesday:

I'm glad you're enjoying the beaches, they are beautiful. Please don't be offended by the small-mindedness of the minority. Most people round here have a 'live and let live' mentality. I *know better than anyone that life is too short to not enjoy it, to not do the things that you want to do or to be held back by worries over what other people will think.*

I agree with Annie. It was a bit of a shock when I came in to clean today and found you guys wandering around naked, but only because I wasn't expecting it. Don't let anyone tell you how to live your life.
  Sophia

Thank you both for your understanding.

Back to the beach again today. At least we were with our own sort of people there. You do get the spectators though, the ones that just go just to have a look. The sun was really hot today and we had to protect ourselves with liberal amounts of sun cream. That is the only downside of being a naturist; there is more exposed skin that could get burned.

Wednesday:
Another day on the beach today. A few meerkats in the dunes today, the spectators that keep popping their heads over the dunes to have a look at us. We could hear them giggling. But we can cope with the giggling; it's the rudeness that upsets us. The other naturists are all very friendly.

Thursday:
We are going home today but we will definitely be back. Everyone has been very friendly.

⸎

4th to 8th September
Hetty O'Donahue (yay!!!)

Hello, my dear, it's good to see you too. I was worried when you left Wales so hurriedly last time, but I was relieved to get your phone call to say that everything was OK. I've been dying of curiosity ever since.

It was horrible of Oliver to tell you Willow Cottage had burned down, but you can't shut him out of your life over it. He's your best friend, what on earth is going on between you two?

In short, the man is being a total arse. He doesn't want me to see other men, but he doesn't want me either. He still feels really guilty over Nick's death and it's messing him up spectacularly.

Why does he feel so guilty over the accident? I don't know the details of what happened that night, just that Nick died in a car crash. Is there something that Olly did that he should feel guilty over?

No. The roads were icy, a car coming the other way took a corner too quickly, lost control and slammed into them. Olly escaped with minor injuries, Nick was killed instantly. There was nothing Olly could have done. By all accounts he was driving slowly because of the ice. I can't even blame the other driver. We've all been there and lost control in icy conditions. But there is absolutely no blame to be laid on Olly's shoulders.

So now he thinks he shouldn't benefit from Nick's death by being with you?

I don't think he wants me that way. He's never showed any interest in me like that.

You slept together, that shows some level of interest.

It shows he was drunk and horny.

Don't be blind and stubborn. You just have to read some of his messages in this book. God, a seven-year-old girl could even see it when she saw you two together. It's clear he's not doing anything because of his love and loyalty for Nick.

Are you looking forward to your birthday meal in The Frog? Everyone is coming. I believe Simon and Leila have ordered a hog roast. William is coming too. He's bought a new suit for the occasion.

Ah that's sweet of him and yes, of course, I'm looking forward to seeing everyone. But you don't get away with it that easily. I have to ask, what did Nick leave you in the will?

Urgh! Nothing. There was nothing that he could leave to me, everything we owned was owned equally. It wasn't what he left me that upset me, it was what he left for Olly. I do love Nick, but he had a foolish, sentimental heart.

What did he leave Olly?

Nick's happiness.

Oh.

Have you told him?

No of course not. It wasn't Nick's to give away. I don't want Olly to take it just because Nick has told him to, or out of guilt or loyalty.

Friday:
Going to see William now. He makes me smile. He's like putting on an old, comfortable, favourite sweater. Since Oliver has paid for William to have help with the farm, there's no need for him to get up and work on the farm every day. But still he does. He loves the cows and won't be parted from them. It's incredibly endearing.

Just got back from spending a few hours at the farm. William is very shy and sweet. He gets so flustered around me.

Saturday:
The day of the big party. Sixty years. It has gone by so quickly. I have had a fantastic varied life so far. After marrying Robert forty years ago, we lived in Malaysia for three years and China for two. I gave birth to three beautiful children. We lived in New York in a huge apartment overlooking Central Park.

We finally settled here in Chalk Hill and raised our family here, where Robert had been raised himself. We spent twenty glorious years here, and I know the friends I have here have been and always will be the best friends I could ever hope for.

I have been a secretary, a double-glazing salesperson, a teacher, a bingo-caller and opened my own cake shop. I have worked in a supermarket and even had a brief stint as a weather girl on local TV.

The kids grew up and moved away. When our eldest, Claire, had children of her own, we moved to Tenby to be closer to the grandkids. A few years later, they moved to the furthest shores of Scotland, but we had found our home there and decided to live out our retirement overlooking the beach.

My best friend and soul mate was taken from me five years ago, which was the lowest point of my life. But with the help of my dear friends, my family and my eight fantastic grandkids, I made it through the other side. Even my friends from here rallied round and William, Sophia, Albert, Mary and Steve would often drive the seven hours to Tenby to keep me company. I would have been lost without them.

I have had six dogs and three cats. I have worked my way through twelve, no thirteen, cars of varying colours, manoeuvrability, speed and coolness.

I have ridden on the backs of horses, elephants, camels and even a cow. I have driven a Harley Davidson, a snow mobile, a tank and a motor-powered sofa. I have fired a rifle, flown in a hot air balloon over the Serengeti and scuba-dived on the Great Barrier Reef. I have learned to ski, wakeboard and throw a pot on a potter's wheel.

I have been to Vegas, Hollywood, Russia, Iceland, Hong Kong and sat on Santa's lap in Lapland.

And now I've reached my twilight years, is it time for me to hang up my weather-beaten walking boots and take it easy? Not likely. Sixty is not the end. There is still life in the old dog yet and a whole lot more world to see.

I intend to marry a rich, virile, young toy-boy and travel the world with him, until I die with a glass of tequila in one hand and a Mexican sombrero in the other.

Oh, Hetty, that's beautiful. If I live half the life that you have when I reach your age I'll be happy.

I want to travel the world too. I've thought about this a lot over the last few weeks and I've decided to sell up and travel for a while. I'm selling Willow Cottage as a successful business, and my house next door. It's going to take a few months for it all to go through, but I've already started to put the wheels in motion. Would you like a travelling companion for a while? I'm not a rich, virile, hot young man but I still think we can have some fun.

I would like that. I'd like that a lot.

Well, I'd best get my party dress on. Maybe we can both find some hot young men tonight to accompany us on our travels.

Have had the best night. All my children came, even though they said they couldn't make it, and my beautiful grandchildren, who are growing up so fast. My friends from distant shores were there as were all the local ones too. Fairy lights were strung across the beer garden and all the benches pushed back to form a dance floor. I have not sat down all night. I have danced and laughed and talked and danced some more. The food was superb, the company was even better. I am feeling a tiny bit tipsy now, what with all the champagne and cider.

Amongst all the dancing and laughter there is one moment that stood out for me, the highlight of my night. Until now I didn't even think I wanted it. But my heart seemed to know better.

William and I were dancing. I had pretty much danced with everyone, so it didn't strike me as weird that I was dancing with him. But as the song ended, he held onto me a little bit longer. And then he uttered seven little words to me. Seven words I never thought I'd hear, seven words I never wanted to hear until he said them. 'I like you, Hetty, I really do.' Then he kissed my head and left. My heart hasn't stopped pounding since.

Sunday:
I told you he liked you.

Don't get too excited. It was just the drunken ramblings of a lovely, sweet man who is fond of me and then me getting all slushy and sentimental after one too many glasses of champagne last night. I wouldn't buy your wedding hat just yet. Besides, as I said before, I want to travel the world. I've done the settling down bit for the last twenty years or more. I've got a need to see the sights. William would never leave his cows.

For you he might. Men do strange things for love.

Like telling someone their house has burnt down so they will come home? Like spending six months holding that someone in their arms because they can't bear to be parted from them?

Grief and stubbornness, not love, Hetty. You have a reason to stay here, at least for a little while, long enough to persuade William to see the world with you. I have nothing for me here anymore.

Don't underestimate the importance of friendship and family.

I would never underestimate that. My friends here are wonderful, William and Sophia especially. But they will always be a part of my life, no matter where in the world I am. I feel

125

like I need a fresh start. Everywhere I go here is filled with memories of Nick and Olly and I can't have either of them.

I get that. Coming back here always reminds me of my years with Robert and Tenby is also filled with memories. A fresh start can be a good thing.

Monday:
Thanks for your part in organising the birthday party. I'll be back in a few weeks. It's William's birthday so... I'll see you then and we can make plans for our world domination.

⊱

12th to 15th September
Rosie and Jake Hamilton

Hi, guys, looking forward to seeing you again. Dinner tonight at my house?

Hi Annie,
 It's so good to be back, we missed you too. Dinner sounds lovely.
 Rosie xx

Hi Annie,
 No potent cider tonight please. We are trying for a baby.
 Jake

Trying, no luck so far. ☹

There's no rush, my love.

Lovely dinner at Annie's tonight. Now to try for a baby, again.

No pressure then. Nothing like a romantic weekend away, and this is nothing like a romantic weekend away.

Stop writing in this book and get upstairs.

Saturday:
Going for a walk on the beach now.
  Rosie

I've been allowed out of the bedroom for good behaviour.

We found a puppy on the beach, obviously a mongrel, some kind of terrier/Jack Russell cross by the look of it. A bundle of white fur, floppy ears and large paws, he is so cute. There didn't appear to be anyone nearby that he belonged to. We're looking after him for the weekend and Annie is going to ask around to see if anyone has lost him. Hopefully we can find his owners before we go home.

We've called him Dash; all he does is run around like he's got a firework up his bum. He is so friendly.

He seems to adore Annie; she certainly has a way about her. Everyone loves her. Jake and I were looking forward to seeing her as much as seeing the beautiful beaches.

Dash has little or no discipline; no wonder he ended up alone, he won't do anything he's told. Makes me smile though, he's such a little bugger.

I never thought I'd be saying this, but I'm relieved that Dash's arrival has given me a reprieve from all the sex. I was honestly going to feign a headache tonight. Sex for fun is one thing, sex to make a baby is a whole other ball game. No pun intended.

You said you wanted a baby too.

I do. Of course I do. But I kind of wanted to enjoy the baby-making process too. If we get stressed out about it, it's never going to happen.

What if it never happens?

Of course it will. We've only been trying for a few months. If we are still having problems conceiving after Christmas, we can go and see the doctor about it. For now, we just need to relax and enjoy our time together.

Sunday:
Dash ended up sleeping with us last night. He howled when we left him alone downstairs and it was easier to have him sleep with us, at least then we were able to sleep for a few hours. It doesn't bode well for when we have kids. Rosie loves him, she carries him around everywhere, it's so cute to see.

I think I might actually be in love. It's so lovely to watch Dash run across the beach, his tail doing cartwheels, his paws too big to run gracefully. I could watch him all day.

Still no sign of his owner. Is it wrong that I'm a little bit happy about this?

We can't keep him, Rosie, you know that.

Monday:

I'm gutted to leave Dash, but after long discussions with Jake, I know it's not practical to take him home with us. His owners could still be around somewhere and Annie can help reunite him easier than we can. Plus we live in a fourth-floor flat, we don't even have a garden for him to run around in and the little tyke needs some space to burn off his endless energy. He'd be on his own for hours whilst we were at work too. At least we know Annie will take really good care of him, she seems to have fallen for him as much as we have. And if his owners can't be found, we can always come back and visit him whenever we can.

You are welcome back any time; Dash will miss you guys too.

⋇

16th to 18th September
Judy Fisher

Tuesday:
I was supposed to be here yesterday, but I've broken my ankle and had to wait for my son to drive me down today. Though I can hobble around, I'm more or less housebound. I didn't want to miss this weekend, I've been looking forward to it for ages - but I hope I don't get bored by being stuck in the house.

There was a bit of a mix-up with the keys when I arrived. I spoke to Annie Butterworth yesterday and she said she would be here to meet me when I arrived today. When I got here she was nowhere to be found. Finally a lady called Sophia spotted me and she had a spare key to let me in. She was very concerned that Annie was not here. She said that maybe she had taken Dash for a walk.

The plot thickens. Someone called Sally came round last night for a pre-arranged cup of tea, but Annie wasn't in.

Something is very wrong with this Annie's disappearance. Apparently there was a suicide note left in the house. I heard Sophia talking to someone called Olly about it when she phoned him from the end of Annie's garden. Sophia had the note in her hand and read it to him. The note said something like 'Dear Olly, I can't go on like this anymore. It has to end now.' He made her read it twice, which was handy for me.

I don't mean to sound callous, obviously I'm concerned for her, but I feel like I've stepped into an episode of Coronation Street. It's surprising what you can glean just from listening to one side of a conversation. Apparently Olly and Annie had a big row the last time he was here. Sophia said that after he had left Annie was miserable for days. Sophia said Nick, I think that's Annie's dead husband, had left a will and that had upset Annie too. Olly is obviously on his way up here now as Sophia said she would wait for him before she did anything.

Good Lord, this is the most exciting weekend I've ever had. A few minutes ago, a sleek black helicopter landed in the field out the back and who steps out? Only bloody Oliver Black, the sexy author whose every book has been made into some huge budget Hollywood-type film. I had no idea that the Olly that Sophia had been talking to was the Oliver Black. How has he got involved with some nobody from the middle of nowhere? He always seems to be on

130

the arm of a different woman every week when I've seen him in these gossip mags, all beautiful, stunning, glamorous women. Though recently, I recall, he has been linked with the actress Vivienne Lake. I wonder what she makes of this impromptu visit to this tiny village. I can only assume this Annie Butterworth must be some gorgeous model. Oliver Black is much more beautiful in real life, so tall and powerful.

Sophia and Oliver have been talking in the garden. Sophia was really angry with him. She said that Oliver might as well have died that night if he wasn't going to live his life anymore. Then she talked about Nick, and how he would have hated seeing Oliver like this and hated even more what Oliver was doing to Annie. She showed him what I can only presume was Nick's will. Oliver groaned when he read it and then said he had to find Annie.

People have started to amass on the village green, easily a hundred people or more.

Suddenly the arrival of a dog amongst them has caused a great upheaval. Apparently this is Dash, Annie's dog, and he was covered head to toe in mud. Though if they were hoping Dash would turn out to be some Lassie-type hero and lead them to Annie's body, they were sadly mistaken. He chased a squirrel up a tree, hounded a pigeon and was only stopped from running across the road by the local constabulary.

Oliver Black seems to be organising the troops; they've split off into little groups in search of the body. Many have headed for the beach, Annie's favourite place, though the general consensus is that, judging by the state of the dog,

131

she must be in the salt marshes which is a dangerous place, especially when the tides come in. Now we have a race against the clock, it's brilliant - I mean, obviously very worrying for all concerned.

The village of Chalk Hill has gone quiet. A few elderly people are manning the home front in case Annie comes back, but everyone else has gone out looking for her.

I've just noticed a piece of paper on the table in Annie's garden, presumably the unappreciated will. Shall I sneak next door and get it?

I keep walking past the window and staring at this piece of paper. It flutters gently in the wind, teasing me, tempting me.

I can't bear it; I have to know what's in it.

Curiosity got too much for me, I've just retrieved it. It doesn't say much, nothing that I can see would cause Annie to get upset. Nick is obviously something of a poet as he leaves Olly the gift of happiness, but he talks about it like happiness is a solid thing to hold and keep.

> **To Olly. In the event of my death I want you to have my happiness. I want you to know that feeling of sheer, unadulterated bliss and joy. I have that. I wake up every day and find myself wrapped in it. Every time I hold my happiness in my hands, my heart feels fit to burst, my face aches with smiling so much. I want you to have that happiness too. Take it now with my complete and utter blessing. Grab it with both hands and**

never let it go. Look after my happiness, cherish it and love it and be happy too.
   Nick

Weird. Surely in the last words to his loved ones he would be more explicit and just say where he had hidden his stash of gold instead of this vague message about happiness. Who wants happiness anyway, gold is much more fun.

That's probably why Annie is upset, because there is no hidden treasure and she thought there would be.

The sun is already setting and the search party is yet to return.

She's been found, though I don't know if she is alive. Someone is bringing her back now, but the oldies looked very worried.

A Land Rover has just pulled up outside. Oliver Black got out looking filthy and, incredibly, sexier than ever. He rushed round to the passenger side, but a blonde was already getting out. It must have been Annie because they went into her house together. She was pretty, but nothing to write home about. Certainly nothing that would compare to the beauties Oliver normally hangs around with. She was filthy and moved stiffly, like she was in pain, but certainly no lasting injuries. Oliver tried to help her into the house but she pushed him away. I wouldn't push him away if he had his arm round me like that.

Oliver and Annie seem to be having some big argument. Her back door is open and so is mine, though I can only catch a few bits. It's clear though that she wants him and he doesn't want her. She obviously wanted to commit suicide because he turned her down and now he's here because he feels guilty about that. But seriously though, who does she think she's kidding, like she'd have any chance with the great Oliver Black. The man is a god.

She is denying that she tried to commit suicide. She claims the note she wrote to Olly about it all coming to an end was the beginning of a letter she started writing to him weeks ago but never finished. She is trying to put the blame on her dog, Dash, who apparently broke his lead and ran into the salt marshes. She ran after him and fell down a ditch and couldn't get back out. Likely story. Oliver doesn't seem to believe her either.

Now that Annie is safe, I wonder if it would be a good time to go round and ask for his autograph.

They've just had sex!!! This really is better than Coronation Street. Her downstairs bathroom is next to mine and there is a hole near the floor that I can see through. I saw a chink of light coming through it earlier today, so when I heard her saying she was going for a shower and he offered to help her, I knew I had to take a sneaky peek. Lying down on the floor with my dodgy ankle was a bit tricky but totally worth it.

She was naked by the time I looked and Oliver was washing her hair. He was still wearing his trousers, more's the pity, but his body is beautiful. He started washing her body and the whole time she had her eyes closed, her hands by her side as if she would rather be anywhere but there. If I was being washed by Oliver Black, I would grab him and shove my tongue down his throat, rip those trousers off and have sex with him against the shower wall.

The next thing, Oliver's hands are on her breasts, which elicited the first reaction from her since they'd got into the shower. When she asked what he was doing, he told her he was taking what was rightfully his. This provoked an even bigger reaction; she pushed him away and tried to get out the shower but he stopped her, she fought against him and he pinned her against the wall with her hands above her head. I thought he might rape her, but then he told her that he thought he was going to come up here and find her dead, that it terrified him and he needs to know she is alive, he needs to feel her heart beating next to his.

She's obviously a very clever girl. She threatens to commit suicide which gets him running back up here, then tries to pretend she's not interested in him which would obviously damage his male pride. He practically has to beg to sleep with her, rather than her pouncing on him. Very clever indeed. I don't think I would be that subtle.

He kissed her throat, still pinning her to the wall and when he kissed her on the mouth, she kissed him back. And the next thing, they're having sex, right against the shower wall.

It was hard and fast and urgent and passionate and I couldn't take my eyes off them for a second.

After, they were on the floor kissing for ages as the hot water poured over them and just as I was starting to get a bit bored by the kissing, they had sex again. This time it lasted much longer and was slower, more languid, his hands were all over her as if he couldn't get enough of her. They kissed nonstop throughout. The man really is a god.

Finally, when they finished, Oliver got up straight away. Annie started saying he couldn't leave again like last time, that they'd done nothing wrong. Oliver came back to her and wrapped her in her robe and then scooped her up like

135

she weighed nothing. He told her he wasn't leaving, that he was never leaving her again and he was simply taking her to bed.

I just ran, or rather hobbled, out to the garden and I could see them in Annie's bedroom window. They were both naked, well at least from the waist up, and he was kissing her, just before he turned out the light.

It's gone quiet next door now. I can't wait till tomorrow.

Wednesday:
Another row woke me up. Though I really couldn't hear the specifics at all this time. Vivienne was mentioned, the conveniently forgotten fiancé. I think he hit her. I could hear thuds and screams; a glass was broken or thrown. Not long after that, the helicopter arrived and he left.

The press have arrived, there are maybe fifty of them camped outside Annie's house. I wonder if this has anything to do with the few phone calls I made. I told them what I had seen and heard, which they seemed very interested in. I can't wait to hear Annie's version of events. After the way he treated her this morning, she is going to rip him to shreds.

They were all over Annie when she stepped out of her house. He had obviously hit her because her face looked swollen and she had bruises on her arms. To my surprise she denied that there was an incident yesterday over her attempted suicide, or that she and Oliver had ever had any kind of relationship or that they'd had a row that morning. They asked her about the bruises and she said she had fallen over whilst walking the dog. She confirmed that Oliver had been there, but that he often pops up this way to visit his dad and aunt and will often check in on her too as she was married to his brother. She said they were best friends growing up and that hasn't changed. I can't believe she would stick up for him after he treated her so badly this morning. When asked about how his long-term girlfriend Vivienne Lake would feel about his visit, she said that she had met Vivienne on many occasions and that Vivienne knew that Annie's and Oliver relationship stretched to nothing more than friendship. She said that she hopes Oliver and Vivienne have a very long and happy relationship together. If Vivienne does believe her, more fool her.

Once the press speak to the locals, they'll at least know the truth about Annie's attempted suicide, if nothing else.

To my upmost annoyance, the locals have denied everything. When asked what happened yesterday with the mass search party, every single one of them has looked confused as if they didn't remember the six hours they were out looking for her in the cold and rain.

Vivienne Lake has tweeted that she knew that Oliver was coming here for the night to see friends and family and that Annie is a very close friend to them both. A close friend that has stabbed Vivienne in the back.

Oliver has also tweeted that it must be a slow day in the news office for them to be rehashing two-year-old stories. Apparently the press were all over him when he stayed with Annie after Nick died, and he can't see how a quick visit to his family and sister-in-law could possibly be so riveting to the press.

Oliver has just tweeted again that he is going to the dentist now if any of the press are interested in that, maybe it will make front-page news.

Oliver has just tweeted that he has had a ham sandwich for lunch and expects to see it on News at Ten tonight.

Annie is in her front garden tending to the weeds. The press are losing their enthusiasm for the story now, they've taken a few half-hearted shots of her doing the garden, but with no one to confirm the story I just look like some mad, nosy old bat with too much time on her hands.

Thursday:
After the locals all closed ranks and denied anything was untoward, the press have all left. My son is coming to pick me up soon. Despite the fact that I've been made to look like an idiot, I have had the best weekend. I'll be back again soon to catch up on more gossip.

Judy Fisher has just left and she'll be coming back over my dead body, which won't be any time soon because I did not try to kill myself!!! I can't believe that every detail of my life has been printed here in black and white for every guest to read. Especially as most of it is completely inaccurate. I'd like to categorically state that Oliver did not hit me.

Nor did we have sex.

Oh my!! This makes for an interesting read.

Sophia!! Nothing happened; this is just the inane babble of a bored and lonely madwoman. You know Oliver would never hit me. How much more of Judy's messages do you think are completely made up?

138

There's no smoke without fire.

There's no fire!

Your red cheeks and the gleam in your eye would suggest otherwise.

~

19th to 22nd September
Mr and Mrs Jones

Mr and Mrs Jones? Really? Come on, Anthony, is that the best you could do?

The secrecy is driving me mad. The separate mobile phones, the seedy hotels, the secret liaisons. And what's the point? Everyone knows, your boss knows, your friends know, your parents know, I wouldn't be the least surprised if your wife knows.

Do you think Annie Butterworth really cares who we are? Do you think she's going to ring your wife and tell her we're having a sordid affair? Quite frankly I'd be relieved if she did. Your marriage is a sham and the sooner it's over the better.

My darling Rachel, I love you, you know that. We will be together soon, without all this secrecy. I'm just not willing for that bitch Jessica to have grounds for divorce. She'll take me for every penny I have and there's no way I'm letting her have it. Be patient, I have a plan.

Does your plan involve having your cake and eating it? Does it involve you being a spineless coward?

OK, I can see you're in a bad mood. Is it because my secretary called you a whore?

That's part of it. You did nothing to defend me? You should have sacked her on the spot.

Rachel, Mrs Kessington has worked for my company for thirty-five years, she's a diamond and I couldn't possibly sack her. Yes, she speaks her mind, but I'd be lost without her. And I could hardly defend you, could I? What would you have me tell her? This is the woman I love and want to spend my life with?

So you'd rather she thought I was a whore? Some cheap tart you picked up from a street corner?

I'd rather she didn't know about you at all, but since you insist on turning up at my office at regular intervals, what do you expect? Besides, it pays to keep her on side. She plays golf with Mrs Axe on a regular basis, Jessica's mother. I do not want anything getting back to Jessica.

I was mortified.

Are we going to communicate through this damned book all weekend? If I'd wanted the cold shoulder, I could have stayed at home with my wife.

Saturday:
I'm feeling much happier now. My god, the man is good with his hands.

Rachel! Good lord! Why don't we just video our antics and leave a copy for future guests to watch. I do not want to see this kind of thing in this book again.

140

I didn't come on this weekend to enjoy nice walks on the beach. I came for one reason only. If I can't write about that, then I have nothing more to say.

Sunday:
I still have nothing to say, because we've done nothing else but that.

Monday:
Mmm, I like doing nothing. In fact, I could do nothing for the rest of my life with this man. Nothing in the kitchen, nothing in the lounge, nothing on the dining table, nothing in the bedroom, I loved doing nothing in the shower and even late last night we did nothing in the garden.

We're going home today. I'm sure going to miss doing nothing for a while.

⁓

27th September to 4th October
Gaby and Seth Jacobs

A lovely week planned with my lovely wife.

We haven't spent any real quality time with each other for a long while and I think it's time we did.

In truth, we haven't been getting on that well lately.

My counsellor says I need to be truthful with her, that if this week achieves nothing else, I must talk to her honestly, to tell her exactly what I'm feeling. It's so hard to talk to her when she barely looks at me, when we've hardly spoken at all in the last few months. So maybe I can be truthful here first.

I'm scared I'm losing her.

Gaby miscarried about a year ago. She was five months' pregnant and we lost him. A little boy. We were going to call him Jack. God, it still breaks my heart to think of it. Afterwards Gaby fell into a deep depression. She cried almost nonstop for a month. It hurt me so much that I could do nothing to take away this pain. But despite what we had been through, what we had lost, we still stayed close. Intimately, physically and emotionally. Our counsellor warned that this death could tear us apart but, if anything, we were closer than ever.

She started to come round, to smile again. She stopped seeing our counsellor, although I continued to do so. She said being with him reminded her of a bad time in her life and she wanted to move on. For six months she was the woman I fell in love with again. We laughed, we danced, we went out, we saw friends, we made love every night. Then she fell pregnant again and everything changed. She is four months' pregnant now. It should have been the happiest four months of our lives. Instead it has been the worst.

She's started crying again, not during the day, but at night when we lie in bed together.

Where before she was perfectly comfortable with her body, she's now taken to hiding herself away, covering her body with a towel or robe. I'm not even allowed in the bathroom when she is showering.

I've tried to talk to her about it, but she won't listen. Every time I try to bring it up she walks away.

She's pulling away. There is a void there now where there never was before. Last week she told me if I wanted to leave then I should leave. She said she didn't need me to raise this baby and she would be perfectly fine on her own.

I have never cried so much before in my life.

The thought of losing her is heart–breaking.

I don't know what to do.

This cottage has so many happy memories for us. It's where we met when we came with a bunch of friends five years ago. It's where I brought her when I wanted to propose. I thought maybe we could recapture the magic.

Though the way she has just looked at me makes me wonder if this is really it for us.

I don't know if there is any way back for us now.

Sunday:
Have asked Gaby to come for a walk on the beach with me but she's refused. Guess I'll go on my own.

Seth plays the poor husband very well. He is not going to pin this breakdown on me. All this is his fault.

I knew you blamed me for our baby's death. You always denied it but I knew you did.

I don't blame you for that. I might hate you right now, but I could never hate you for that.

You hate me? And you decide that writing it in this book is the best medium to declare that?

You decided that this book was the best medium to tell everyone that I had a miscarriage and about my depression. I hate you for that right now. What's between us is between us. Why you insist on seeing that overpaid counsellor every week to tell him all our problems I don't know. If you have a problem with me you should tell me.

I've tried to talk to you, you won't listen. You've barely said a word to me for four months.

So you do have a problem with me?

No, of course not. You won't speak to me, you cry all the time. I don't know what I've done wrong.

Are you having an affair?

Oh my God, no! How could you think that?

I don't know what's worse, you falling out of love with me because there's someone else, or because you've just grown bored of me.

I haven't fallen out of love with you. I love you so much.

I see it in your eyes every day. You don't want to be with me anymore.

Monday:
I want a divorce. I'm so miserable, you're making me so miserable and I can't go on like this.

Wait. Wait a minute. We need to talk about this, properly.

There's nothing to talk about. There is no future for us anymore.

You need to think about this.

I've thought about it, for two months. Don't fight this please. Don't make it harder than it already is. This is what you wanted.

How can you say that? I want you, I want to be with you. Please don't do this. Tell me what I can do to change your mind, what is it that I'm doing that makes you so miserable?

I'm not going to change my mind. And it's more a case of what you're not doing.

I don't understand. Please talk to me about this. I deserve some kind of explanation. I can't lose you, I love you.

No you don't, not anymore.

You've said more in this book in the last few days than you have to me in the last few months. Talk to me.

The book doesn't hate me.

I don't hate you. God, Gaby, please.

It's late. I'm going to bed. I would prefer it if you slept in the spare room tonight.

Tuesday:
Just popped by to see if you guys are settling in OK, it's been very quiet.

Just read your previous messages. I'm so sorry you guys are having problems. I won't intrude; you need some time to talk this through. It seems like there is still a lot of love there worth fighting for. Talk to each other; if it is going to end, then part honestly and openly with each other.
   Annie x

Thanks, Annie.
I haven't slept a wink. I'm trying to trace it back to when it all went wrong. We were so happy.

Then I got fat. Now you think I'm hideous.

You're pregnant, not fat. And you are so beautiful.

You always had a thing about my body; you said how beautiful I was. You could never keep your hands off me. Now you won't even touch me. You find me repulsive. I saw it in your eyes when I told you I was pregnant again. You were disappointed. You didn't want me to get fat again.

No, Gaby. I wasn't disappointed. I was thrilled. But terrified at the same time. I was so scared that we would lose our baby again, that you would be sad again. It tore me up that you got so sad last time and there was nothing I could do to stop it. But worse than that, I was the reason for it.

You were not the reason our baby died. Do you still honestly believe that? The doctors told you it wasn't your fault, I've

146

told you, and even the overpaid counsellor told you it wasn't your fault. Making love to me the night before did not cause me to miscarry. You have to let this go.

How can I? You're leaving because you hate me? If you don't hate me over that, then what?

YOU'RE NOT LISTENING TO ME!!! I'M LEAVING BECAUSE YOU DON'T LOVE ME ANYMORE, BECAUSE YOU FIND ME SO UGLY YOU CAN'T BEAR TO TOUCH ME.

I'm going to bed. Please sleep in the spare room again. I can't sleep in the same bed with you anymore, feeling so grotesque and fat.

My darling Gaby. I can't believe you have thought that for the last few months. I wanted to touch you, to make love to you so much. You have always turned me on and you being pregnant has absolutely not changed that. If anything, the feelings I have for you have intensified.

The first time I stopped you from making love to me, I knew you were pissed off, but I didn't realise you thought it was because I didn't love you anymore. I thought you knew how scared I was of it happening all over again; I thought you understood my fears.

We should have talked about it, I tried. But every time I did, you would just walk away. I should have made you listen, but when you get in your moods it's always best to leave you to calm down. You've told me that on many occasions, to just leave you when you get crabby. I thought it would last a few days. But I didn't realise it would last for so long. The more I left it, the worse it got.

Gaby, the reason I haven't made love to you is because I was so scared of hurting the baby, of hurting you.

Wednesday:
Gaby came downstairs this morning, read my previous message and burst into tears. She sobbed for about half an hour and nothing I said could stop her. Then she got up and walked out.

She's been gone about an hour now. I'm going to try and find her.

I've just got back; Seth is still out looking for me.

Seth, I'm so sorry… I don't know what else to say. We have always been so great in the bedroom, that was one of the best things about our relationship, the sex was amazing. And every time I would look in your eyes and see how much you loved me… To see you turn away from me, to see fear in your eyes instead of love. I thought you hated me, that you had fallen out of love with me. I thought you were only staying because of the baby. I walked away from talking to you because I was so scared you were going to end it and I couldn't bear to hear you say those words. God, I have missed you so much. I didn't realise how much the intimacy meant to me, but I need you. I can't get through the next five months without you.

I'm going upstairs, and when you get back I want you to come up and make love to me. Please.

Friday:
We have spent the last two days making love, crying, talking and making love. I can't believe we got so close to throwing it all away quite simply because we didn't talk about it. We have promised each other that whatever is going on in our lives, we will always talk it through from now on.

I've been such an idiot and I nearly lost my best friend because of it.

Saturday:
Going for a walk on the beach with my lovely husband before we go home. Thank God we came.

❧

6th to 10th October
Oliver ~~Butterworth~~ Black

Monday:
I'm supposed to be writing my autobiography. I've been putting it off for ages, but it makes sense to write it here, where I grew up.

Why is it harder to write about myself than it is to make up stories?

Flicking back through Judy Fisher's messages has made me laugh. Her writing is more of a work of fiction than any of my previous stories. Me and Annie did not have sex, we did not row and I definitely did not hit her. We had a nice little chat the last time I was here and we agreed to be friends, nothing more.

Tuesday:

Wednesday:

Thursday:

Friday:

Why are you not writing anything?

What would you have me write? I am certainly not going to write down my thoughts and feelings for all to read in this book.

You could write about your week.

My week has been pretty bloody spectacular as it happens.

It is always good to come home and see friends and family.

I have had a pretty good week too.

How's the autobiography going?

I've had a busy week, I've not written much.

Writer's block?

Distractions. Good distractions, very, very good distractions.

I'll see you next week, I have to get this bloody autobiography finished and as I've barely started, I'll be back again on Monday. I'm seeing Vivienne tonight. We're having a nice romantic weekend away.

How lovely. I'm so glad things are going well for you two. I hope she didn't believe the rubbish about us that was in the papers last week.

She knows better than to believe what is written by the paparazzi.

Take care, Annie

❧

10th to 13th October
Arnold Smythe

I'm here because of the conspiracy. Annie Butterworth denied all knowledge of this conspiracy when I just spoke to her, but I have found this tactic across the country and have come to expect it now. Of course the locals know something, how could they not? But they close ranks; they've been paid or threatened by government officials or the military and when people come asking, they just play dumb.

I know differently, of course, they can't hide it from me. Someone has to open the public's eyes. Only death will silence me. They've tried twice to kill me, but I won't lie down. And even in death my legacy will continue.

It seems my mission has support. My website has had over two hundred thousand hits. Even one of the national newspapers ran an article about me. Admittedly it wasn't very complimentary, but I gained a lot of attention after that. Many people wrote to me to say they agreed with my theories.

I have written down my findings and stored them in a safe deposit box, so that even after my death others can continue my fight. I'll write down some of what I know here, the one place they'll never think of looking.

It all started when I was perusing Google Earth and found that many areas were blacked out. Areas had suspicious clouds over them, were heavily pixelated, had black squares over the top of them, were painted green or, in the case of a number of places, a section of another area had just been copied and pasted over the top.

There are many theories as to why this has been done. Extra-terrestrials are one of them. Maybe these places are where aliens have landed and have perhaps created their own town. Extra-terrestrial beacons are another such theory. Nuclear-testing facilities, military bases, royal family homes, the homes of the rich and famous. Whatever it is, it is clear that the powers that be are hiding something from us.

I started to think about what our own government was hiding from us. On one trip to Scotland I found something. I was out hiking near Ullapool and got a bit lost. Using my phone, I was able to pinpoint my location. But then I noticed something weird. There was a small island out in the sea that did not appear on my map. The map indicated that there should only have been sea in my location, but this island, approximately a kilometre in length, was very clear to the naked eye. Not only was there a secret island, but it also had buildings on it, one of them a huge warehouse. I stayed and observed the island through binoculars for many hours. I saw many people walking around this facility, but the main focus of interest was around this large warehouse.

I got a bit lost again walking back, but eventually found a pub. When I asked about the mysterious island, the locals acted as if I was talking rubbish. One man said I was looking at the wrong part of the map and that Isle De Mitt was a military facility, but clearly identifiable on any map I looked at. He showed me on his phone, but the island he showed me bore no resemblance to the shape of the island I saw.

Another man, a man with a glass eye, beckoned to me and told me about the alien spacecraft that had been found in the hills, that they had taken it to this mysterious island that I spoke of. He told me they had used the technology to build a great spaceship that could travel across galaxies and universes. Now I'm not sure whether this man was a credible witness, but it was clear that this island was hidden from the public and it is my job to let people know.

After I wrote about it on my blog, there were two attempts on my life. The first was when a car crashed into mine at a junction. The driver claimed his light was on green at the same time as mine. He spoke with an accent and my insurance company could find no trace of him with the details he gave me. Obviously a government cover-up.

The second attempt on my life came just three days later. A boat I was supposed to be travelling on to the Orkney Islands sank. Thankfully, that day I'd had a suspicious feeling I was being followed and decided to delay my trip. I bought my ticket and made a show of queuing up for the boat but at the last minute, I hid behind some cargo. The boat left and, later that day, I heard that it had got into difficulty and sank. No one else was hurt, but it could have ended so differently.

After that I knew that I must have been onto something, that they were obviously trying to cover it up with my death. It has been my three-year mission to uncover their secrets. So far I have found seven places in the UK that do not exist on any maps or satellite imagery.

One was a small wood that had a fence around it. On the maps and internet, the area is shown as a plain field. I could not see beyond the first layer of trees, but I walked around the perimeter of the fence and plotted it at roughly five hundred square yards. There is a gate with clear evidence of recent tyre tracks and also evidence of electric cabling entering the compound. Locals denied all knowledge of it with most saying it's just a wood and one person saying that it was just a private garden. That night, camping in a nearby field, I observed through my night-vision goggles a truck loaded with boxes going into this compound and leaving later with the boxes removed. I also heard a humming coming from this area.

The second place I found was a black tower. It had no door, no recognisable way in, but I could hear noise and voices from within the tower. It was hidden amongst the trees so wouldn't show on satellite images, but surely it should be marked on Ordnance Survey maps.

I found a hut down a little dirt track. There were no other buildings for as far as the eye could see in any direction. The hut didn't have windows; it had a very heavy metal door and again did not appear on maps or satellite imagery.

The coast is the worst for hidden secrets. Many islands, rocky islets or even the shape of the coast itself is not really as it is seen on satellite imagery. The government have done it so carefully that you would barely even notice. A few extra metres here, a missed lump there. But it is different. You just have to walk it to see that. There was one such tiny islet that had what appeared to be a telephone aerial on it, but neither the islet nor the telephone tower appear on maps or imagery.

Which is why I find myself in Wells-Next-The-Sea. I have asked for my followers to be vigilant too and to let me know if they see anything unusual. One of them has contacted me to let me know of the anomaly here. You simply have to look at the beaches of Wells-Next-The-Sea,

Holkham Bay and the ones further round the coast near Stiffkey, Morston and Blakeney on Google Maps. You will see many of these suspicious blurs or dark patches where the camera does not seem to have taken the pictures clearly.

I asked Annie Butterworth what she was hiding round here and she looked very guilty, but then quickly denied that she was hiding anything.

I will be checking out these beaches tomorrow myself.

Saturday:

I have spent the day walking up and down the beaches here. It is just as I thought, there are oddities. Sandbanks, tiny islets and the shape of the shoreline all differ slightly from that shown on maps and satellite images. Just what are the government trying to hide?

Sunday:

There has been a suspicious black car parked outside my house since late last night. I think they might have found me. Annie Butterworth no doubt told them I was here and that I was asking questions. I saw a man in Annie Butterworth's back garden. He was dressed in a suit and was speaking into one of those earpieces. I heard him say that he would have to end it soon. When he saw me watching him, he ducked behind a bush.

I've just marched round to Annie Butterworth's house to demand she explain this man to me. She said he was just someone she was doing business with. I told her she couldn't fool me and that if she thought she and her friend were going to kill me in my sleep, they had another think coming. Shortly after, the man got in the black car and left.

Monday:
Another car has arrived outside my house this morning. Two men in suits have got out and gone into Annie Butterworth's house. I think it's time to leave.

Oh dear! You do seem to get the weird ones, Annie.

Aw, Sophia, he was harmless enough. Besides, maybe he has a point.

What about?

The government cover-ups, the secret locations.

The man is clearly insane.

Have you never noticed that the beaches here don't exactly match the maps?

Don't you start.

Hehe!! OK, the man was a bit loopy, OK a lot loopy, but I bet there are things the government are keeping from us.

And what are you keeping from me? Who was the man that stayed over Saturday night?

No one stayed over Saturday night. As I told Arnold, the man, and the two other men on Sunday were people I've been talking to about selling Willow Cottage. The first man came to see me Saturday night and said he was staying here in Chalk Hill. He left his car outside and he came back Sunday morning to continue our chat.

You're still serious about that?

About seeing what the world has to offer for a while? Yes. But you will always be a part of my life, I could never forget you. I'll keep in touch, you know that, and come back to visit often. This is my home, you are my home, and living somewhere else won't change that.

❧

13th to 17th October
Oliver ~~Butterworth~~ Black

What is this about all the strange men in your house?

Well, Arnold Smythe was quite strange. There was nothing strange about the other three men, all respectable, professional men. The one on Saturday night was lovely. OK, he was also very fit too. We're sort of seeing each other. We have been for a few weeks.

In a professional capacity?

Of course!

Tuesday:
Good for you. I'm happy for you. I'm loving the smile on your face lately.

I've had a lot to smile about.

A lot?

Lots and lots.

How was your weekend with Vivienne?

Not good. We've being going through a rough patch recently, as I'm sure you've seen in the papers over the last month or two. This weekend was supposed to be about reconnecting but, unfortunately, it was more disconnected. We've argued constantly. I'm finding it hard to remember what it was that I fell in love with.

I've sort of met someone.

Olly!

I haven't done anything with her, I'm not a complete arse. She's beautiful and funny and ... well, if I'm having feelings for someone else it just didn't seem fair on Vivienne. I had to be honest with Vivienne and say I don't think we should go through with the wedding. I mean, maybe it's just a rough patch and we'll come out the other side and laugh about this in a few years' time, but it didn't seem right to be planning a wedding when I'm thinking of someone else. As you know, we were supposed to be getting married on New Year's Eve, but we've decided to put things on hold for a while. We haven't called our relationship off yet. We're still trying to work at it but... well, we'll see.

And the other woman?

Try to avoid her as much as I possibly can. She's American, so it's a good thing that I'm over here for a few months.

Wednesday:

Thursday:

Friday:

Hi.

Hello.

You're still not writing anything?

It's hard to know what to write.

You're a writer!

What I want to write and what I'm allowed to write are two very different things.

How you doing?

I ache. Every part of me aches.

Why do you ache?

Er... new exercise routine. I've been at it every day this week and last week. I'm exhausted, but that good exhausted feeling you get when you've been down the gym. You know ultimately that it's good for you.

You don't need to lose any weight, Annie, maybe you need to lay off the exercise for a while.

NO! No, it's fun, I love it. And I'm not doing it to lose weight, it's erm... purely to get fitter.

Build your stamina? You probably could do with doing that. Have a rest this weekend and start again next week.

Good idea. Though I will miss doing it this weekend, it's become quite addictive.

I'll see you Monday.

Stay away from strange men.

What about the fit ones?

That's allowed.

Well, the one that you saw Saturday night is allowed, the one that makes you smile, not a string of different fit ones.

Just the one, I promise.

❦

17th to 20th October
Matt, Emily and Mia Taylor

Hi, Annie. Thanks for the bug stuff for the girls, they'll have great fun catching the bugs and looking at them under the microscope. Emily wants to say thank you for the chocolate buttons you left too, though I've said they can have them on Saturday night when we have movie night.

Thank you for your card you sent last year too. Sorry I

didn't reply, I found it hard enough to get out of bed in the morning. The girls were the only thing that kept me going.

Every card said the same thing, how sorry people were, how if there was anything they could do, to let them know. No one understood that my heart had actually stopped beating. You got it though. You've been there. Your card meant so much.

In some ways you probably had it harder. With the girls I had a reason to get up in the morning, I had to pull myself together for them. They were too young to properly grieve and so really there was no time for me to do so. Ice-skating lessons, horse-riding lessons and dance classes continued as normal. I couldn't lie and wallow in self-pity, there was never time. You had no one to live for. How you picked yourself up and carried on when there was no reason to, I'll never know. I completely admire you for that.

Matt

I think you had it worse. To have to explain to your kids that Mummy was never coming home, I don't know how you even began that conversation. And you have done such a wonderful job with them in the last year; they are polite, happy, friendly, beautiful girls. Cara would have been so proud. So many families fall apart after a death in the family and I think you are amazing for keeping yours together on your own.

And I wasn't alone after Nick's death; I had a lot of support from friends. My best friend was the thing I got out of bed for. He gave me something to live for.

Hi, Annie, thanks for the sweets and the bugscope is so cool. It seems weird to be here; the last time we came we were a proper family. Daddy asked if we wanted to come back or whether it would bring back too many sad memories. But we had fun here and me and Mia thought that we could have fun here again. Daddy has been sad since Mummy died. He tries really hard not to show it, but I can see it in his eyes.

You seem happier now than last time we were here. Your eyes aren't sad anymore and you are smiling a lot. I wonder if Daddy will ever be happy again.

Emily

Hi Emily,

It's good to see you all again.

The first year is the hardest. It gets slightly easier after that. Your dad will still love and miss your mum every day, but he will smile again and one day the smile will actually meet his eyes. But he is so lucky to have such wonderful girls in his life. I know your love and hugs will continue to make him smile and make him stronger.

If you want, you and Mia can always come round and play with my new puppy, Dash. I'm trying to train him, but it's not working that well. Maybe you can help me.

Thanks for letting us play with Dash today. He is very cute, he even made Daddy smile for a few seconds.

Saturday:
Time for some quality family time on the beach.

We have had a lovely day at the beach, making sandcastles, eating ice cream and playing in the sea. The girls were teaching me how to body board. I forget sometimes how much fun they are and I need to remember that they need that. I'm so glad we came. In actual fact it has been quite cathartic. We have spent time today talking about Cara and the happy memories we have of this place. We need to remember those too and not just focus on how much we miss her.

Movie night now. *Finding Nemo*, *Lion King* and *Harry Potter and The Goblet of Fire.* We are sharing a big bowl of popcorn and sitting underneath the duvet together on the sofa.

AND CHOKLUT BUTENS.
  MIA XXXXXXX

The girls are in bed now after our marathon movie session. I feel I can breathe here. I think I've been holding my breath for the last year and now I can finally let it go. For the first time today, the pain in my chest has lessened slightly. The girls are a part of that, their continued love and support. Annie is a part of it too. She has been so kind, so supportive. When I've talked to her, she really listens. I think it's as important for me to get some quality time this weekend as it is for me to spend quality time with the girls.

Sunday:
We went to see the seals this morning. The girls and Cara loved it last time we were here, and their enthusiasm for it hasn't waned any. Spent some more time on the beach today. We made sand angels in the wet sand. Cara used to love doing that. Mia said that she thought Mummy would be watching us from heaven and smiling that we did that. If there is a heaven, then I bet she is too.

The girls are in bed now. This weekend has been so good for them. It's been good for us all. I think we will come again, but not wait until next year this time; maybe we can make this a regular event.

I'm enjoying a glass of wine. I haven't drunk anything since Cara died, I didn't want to fall into the trap of thinking that alcohol would take the pain away. The girls need me; they don't need a depressive drunk.

Annie is in her garden, also enjoying a glass of wine. I'll invite her in to share one with me. There is something quite sad about drinking alone.

Monday:
Annie, I'm so sorry about last night. It seems my tolerance for alcohol has completely gone if I'm drunk after just two glasses. I'm sorry I kissed you. You've just been so sweet and you're the only one who really gets what I'm going through. I think I thought, I don't know, that maybe we could help each other. I think I was just feeling a bit needy. I hope this won't affect our friendship.

Daddy! You kissed Annie? Are you two going to get married? Annie is lovely, but I'm not sure I want a new mommy yet.

Honey, no. Me and Annie are not going to get married. I was just feeling a bit sad and reached out to Annie for comfort. We need to talk about this properly.

Matt, I just came round to see if you were OK after last night. Please don't worry about kissing me. Of course it won't affect our friendship.

You are a wonderful, very handsome, sweet and kind man. The way you are with the girls is amazing. Under normal circumstances, I would certainly be kissing you back.

164

I'm sort of seeing someone and although it's very early days, I really think this is the person I'm going to spend the rest of my life with. He has put a huge smile back on my face, one which hasn't really been there for over two years. I love him. I'm sorry. I hope one day you will find the right woman that will put the smile back on your face too.

Emily, I'm sure Daddy has explained this to you, but we are just friends and sometimes friends do hug and kiss each other. I promise you we won't get married. But one day Daddy might find someone he can love again, someone he can marry. I hope you can love her too, because she would have to be very special to deserve someone as lovely as your daddy.

Thanks, Annie. I hope everything works out for you and your man.

Thanks, Annie, we will see you and Dash soon.

I LOVE DASH XXXXXXXXXXXXXXXX

❧

20th – 24th October
Oliver ~~Butterworth~~ Black

What's this? I've been gone for one weekend and already you've been kissing another man. What about the fit man that you are 'sort of' seeing? How do you think he feels about this?

I would hope that he would be mature enough to realise that I didn't kiss Matt; he kissed me, that's two very different things. I would hope that, unlike you, he wouldn't act like a complete child. Matt has lost his wife, and I don't know if you remember what that feels like, the pain of losing someone you love, but I do. I know that after Nick died, I just wanted to be held, to be cuddled, to be stroked, because if I could feel that, then I knew I was still alive. I knew that if there was someone in this world that cared enough for me to hold me in his arms for six months, then there was actually something worth living for. Matt doesn't have that. He has his girls, but it's not the same. Besides you will see, if you bothered to read the rest of Matt's messages, that I said the reason I didn't kiss him back was because I'm in love with the man I'm 'sort of' seeing.

Sorry. I didn't mean… I'm sorry. x

Apology accepted. Now, if you've finished sulking, I have a problem in my bedroom you might be able to help me with.

OK, OK, I'm coming…

Tuesday:
Things are going very well lately. Better than well. The high point of my life.

Things getting better with Vivienne then?

No, sadly that isn't going well.

The sales of your latest book? I see you got excellent reviews for Veiled in Darkness. You must be really pleased.

Yes, I am pleased. Yes, of course that's what I'm talking about.

166

Stop grinning at me or I'll give you something to wipe the smile off your face.

I can't help it, you make me laugh.

How are things with your new man? I haven't met him yet, he does seem to stay away when I'm around. Is he scared of me?

Things are good. He's just very busy.

What is it that he does?

Don't start.

I'm interested.

He's my personal trainer.

Oh, he's the one that's making you ache, making you do all that exercise.

Yep, he makes me work up a sweat.

Urgh, I wish I hadn't asked.

Wednesday:
Saw Annie with a very fit man this morning. Looks like he works out a lot. Wonder if this is her new mystery man.

That was Barney, not so much my new man, more my old one.

He didn't look very old. He looked very, very good-looking.

Barney? Yes he is. But the man I'm with is much better-looking than him.

Better looking than Barney. Good lord, the man must be a god!

Some say so, yes.

I like what you did there.

And in the bedroom my new man is amazing, I doubt Barney could compete.

Sounds like you're only with him because of his body and the sex. There's more to a relationship than that.

You're right. Maybe I'll tell him that the next time I see him. No sex for a month to see if we are compatible in other areas too.

I think that's a bit hasty.

No, it's a wonderful idea. I'm sure as hell going to miss the sex, but if we're going to work then we have to know that we can talk and spend time together that's not just about the physical. Thanks, Olly.

Why are you scowling?

Thursday:
I've cheered up a bit now after our conversation yesterday.

I bet you have.

As Hetty is coming to stay this weekend, for my dad's

birthday, can I stay in your spare room? I'll pay you rent if you like.

You are welcome to stay and you can pay me in other ways. I've got lots of little jobs that need doing around the house. The dining room table needs looking at, as does the shower. The floorboards in front of the fire are a bit wobbly and I still have that problem in the bedroom. The stairs too, I need you to look at the stairs.

The stairs? Really?

Yes!

❧

24th to 27th October
Hetty O'Donahue

I'm here for William's birthday. Not a big one like me, he's only a babby in comparison to my age, so no big party, just a meal out with close family and friends.

He's only two years younger than you; he's hardly a toy boy.

Are you excited to see him?

It's William. He's one of my oldest, dearest friends. I wouldn't say I'm excited.

Really? Last time you were here, he told you he liked you, you seemed pretty excited about that.

OK, I am excited, a bit. But he's hardly going to grab me and kiss me, he's just not the grabbing sort. We're both getting on a bit now, I can't wait another twenty years for him to do something.

You could always grab him.
   Oliver

Oh, Olly, I'm an old-fashioned girl at heart, a girl likes to feel loved, to be wooed. I want to feel that he loves me so much that he will walk over hot coals to tell me, not just shrug and think because we're both single and get on OK we might as well be together.

He does love you, Hetty. But you're right, he's not the grabbing sort.

Like father, like son, eh? When are you going to grab Annie and put aside this nonsense of betraying Nick?

Erm… me and Annie are just friends. She's with someone who she loves and I'm with Vivienne.

Rubbish. You two belong together.

Hetty, I can't tell you much about the guy I'm with, at least not yet, and I wish I could, but I love him and boy did he grab me and show me how much he loved me. You need to hold out for that. Don't settle for William if that's not what the heart wants.

Oi! That's my dad.

I love William dearly, but you should never settle. Life is too short to waste it with someone you don't love. Like you and I, Hetty and William will be friends for ever, nothing will change that, but true love doesn't come around very often. You don't want to miss it when it does come round because you are too busy with the person you settled for.

I wouldn't be settling for William. I love him, I really do, but if I am going to be with him, I need to know that he feels the same way.

You love him?

Oh, shut up.

Annie, was that a dig at me?

Why would it be a dig at you?

About us?

No. There is no us. I'm with my man who I love very much and you're with Vivienne. Plus you also have this other woman who lives in America.

Oh, what a tangled web we weave.

You're a writer; you're supposed to be better than this at keeping track of all the twists and turns in the plot.

My life seems a lot more complicated at the moment. I'm not sure what I am allowed to say and what I'm not.

Then say nothing at all and come and help me with my problem.

The one in the bedroom again.

If you like.

Annie!!!

Have I missed something?

Saturday:
Going for a long walk with Sophia on the beach now. We are not, repeat NOT, going to talk about William.

Yes we bloody well are.

Heading out shortly for William's birthday meal. I've changed my outfit three times. I don't know why I'm so nervous, I'm sure nothing will happen. We'll have our meal, we will all chat and there may be some dancing afterwards. William might look at me wistfully, but that's as far as it will go. So why am I getting butterflies in my stomach?

Sunday:
I, erm... not really sure what to write here. I guess I should be honest and say that the walls between Willow Cottage and mine are very thin. I'm guessing, by the noises I heard last night, that William not only grabbed you and told you he loved you, but he grabbed you several times over.

I'm so happy for you, a little embarrassed, but very, very happy for you.

The walls are thin, aren't they? I felt so sorry for Olly having to lie in your spare room and listen to you and *your new man go at it hammer and tongs. I know you're trying to prove a point to Olly, I guess you're trying to make him jealous, but think how much you are hurting him by carrying on like that. I honestly expected more of you than that.*

And yes, William did tell me he loved me last night. I told him I was going to travel the world and he told me he would come with me. It turns out he does love me more than he loves his cows after all.

Hetty, I'm happy for Annie that she has found someone she loves again, I really am. Nothing has made me happier over the last few weeks than to see Annie walking round with a huge smile on her face. And after accidentally hearing my own dad in the throes of passion last night, I put ear plugs in so I certainly didn't hear Annie and her new man. I'm happy for you too, Hetty, you both deserve it.

I'm flying out to New York tonight for a few days to do some book stuff, so I imagine you'll be gone by the time I get back. Though I'll guess I'll see you soon. You guys aren't thinking of travelling until the new year, are you?

There's stuff to sort out here first, not least our wedding, so it'll probably be March or April before we leave.

Good. Annie has something important to tell you, but I think she will have to sit on it for a few more weeks until things have been finalised.

❧

1st to 8th November
Jessica Axe

I'm not going back. No one can make me.

I found the number for this place amongst my husband's things. I was going to call it to find out what my husband was doing here. Then it all went wrong and when I fled this was the only number I had on me.

I've read my ex-husband's previous messages in this book. Despite hiding under the guise of Mr and Mrs Jones, Anthony's handwriting is very distinctive. I can't believe he brought that whore here, he never took me anywhere.

Urgh! I feel sick that he fucked her on the dining table, in the shower, in the bed.

Coming here was a mistake.

Though I can't go back. I can never go back.

He had a plan; he said so in this book. And I fell for it hook, line and sinker. The plan involved his best friend, Ryan.

I had been so sad for months. Anthony was nasty, snide, constantly attacking me, verbally not physically, though he might as well have hit me for the pain he caused. I can't remember the last time we made love. He stayed out late at work, went away on business at the weekends. Of course I knew he was having an affair, I just couldn't prove it. The more he pulled away and the more he told me I was fat and ugly, the more depressed I became.

Ryan seemed to be my knight in shining armour. He would

174

come round, firstly on the pretext of calling on Anthony when he was away, then he would stay and we would chat. Later he came when he definitely knew Anthony was away. We would chat for hours and he made me feel beautiful again. I had something to live for. But the whole time I was being played.

We slept together. God, I was desperate to be touched, to be loved again. Little did I know that Ryan had videoed the whole thing, that he had been asked to come on to me so that Anthony had grounds for divorce.

You should have seen Anthony's smug face when he served me with the divorce papers. He thought he had won.

I soon wiped the smile off his face. Permanently.

Hi, Jessica. I just came by to see if you are OK. You came here so last minute and you sounded stressed when I spoke to you on the phone a few hours ago.
  Annie Butterworth

I'm fine. Not stressed at all actually.

I feel free.

Good. If you need anything, let me know. Or if you just need to chat...

Sunday.
Crap. My picture is on the news. No story yet about what happened, just that I'm missing and people are worried. Of course I was supposed to be at work Friday and Saturday and I've never called in sick before, let alone just not turned up.

I bet it was that nosy cow Brenda from Human Resources that called the police.

I wonder if they know yet.

Now the police are involved, it won't be long before they find out.

Jessica, I've just seen the news, are you OK?

I'm fine. There's a thing called customer confidentiality. You're not allowed to tell anyone who is staying in your guesthouse. I expect you to keep quiet.

Of course, but if people are worried and the police are looking for you, wouldn't it be better to let them know you are safe? The longer you leave it, the more likely your friends and family will think the worst. No one should go through that kind of worry unnecessarily. You don't have to tell them where you are, just that you are safe so they stop looking. If you want, I can call them.

No!

I won't tell them anything, just that you are safe.

If you would prefer that I didn't, then I won't. I'm not sure what you've run away from, but you're safe here. You can trust me.

Against my better judgement, I've agreed to Annie ringing the police to let them know I'm safe. Maybe this will take some of the heat off me.

At least for a little while.

I'm going to sit next to her when she does it to ensure she doesn't give away any clues to my whereabouts.

The police wanted to speak to me to prove that Annie was telling the truth, though I refused. Annie refused to give our location, just kept reiterating that I was safe. It seems I can trust her. For now at least.

I've told Annie she has to stay here in the house with me for a little while, in case she runs back next door and phones the police again to tell them where I am. Annie has assured me that she won't, but I'd prefer it if she stayed. Annie seems to be taking this in her stride; she says she'll make the spare bedroom up.

I've confiscated her mobile phone.

Monday:
Annie slept peacefully all night. I didn't sleep a wink. I watched her sleep, convinced that if my back was turned, she would sneak out or try to communicate with someone in the village.

I can't let them find me.

The news is still playing the story of me being missing as if they hadn't spoken to Annie yesterday. The police are now urgently asking me to come forward or for anyone who knows my whereabouts to get in touch.

I'm so paranoid that Annie will rat me out that I've tied her to a chair. She put up quite the struggle; she's surprisingly strong for someone so small. I had to knock her out in order to tie her up.

Annie has been unconscious for quite a while now, I hope she's OK.

She finally woke up. She wasn't happy about being tied up. She was talking to me about the police so I gagged her. I need time to think, I don't need her yapping in my ear.

The news is still not saying anything about the murder. I wonder if they have found Anthony's body yet.

I should have hidden it, disposed of it in some way. But I could hardly leave our little redbrick detached house, in our redbrick detached cul-de-sac, with all the Stepford Wives chatting inanely over the garden fence with a dead body under my arm.

Of course I didn't want to kill him. That wasn't my intention. I just wanted to hurt him like he'd hurt me. But there was so much blood. I just panicked and ran.

An interesting development. Oliver Black has just turned up outside Annie's house. He has knocked on her door several times and has now just gone round the back, peering through the windows.

I've never liked him much. He always used to be in the newspapers every week on the arm of a different woman. The papers love him. What happened to loyalty and fidelity? They used to be traits to be valued. So why the papers raise him up to god-like status for being a complete slut, I don't know.

He's been with Vivienne Lake recently, for about two years. Though if I remember rightly, the papers have linked him to his sister-in-law on several occasions and poor Vivienne keeps on taking him back.

Oliver has just texted Annie's phone asking where she is. It seems they know each other.

Just been flicking back through this book and it seems they know each other very well. Whore.

He's just texted her again, telling her to get back to her house quickly because he wants to have her across the dining table.

URGH! He's just sent her three more texts saying what he wants to do to her, each one more crude than the one before.

Bastard! Poor Vivienne looks so sad recently in the papers and all the time he's sneaking around behind her back, fucking Annie Butterworth.

I've just texted him back telling him he's a 'spineless wanker with a very small prick'.

He's just phoned her mobile but, of course, I didn't answer. Though I think he heard the phone ringing in here, because he's just been peering through the windows. Thankfully, the cottage has net curtains so he can't see that Annie is tied to a chair in the kitchen.

So Annie is just like that fucking whore Rachel that Anthony was screwing. The other woman.

I've often wondered about Rachel, whether she knew about me or not. Or whether Anthony played her as well. But there were so many late-night meetings and secret liaisons; I figured she had to know that he was married. Then I thought about what kind of woman would sleep with another woman's husband. What kind of bitch would do that?

Now I have one of those bitches tied up in the kitchen.

Oh, revenge seems sweet indeed.

For all those women that have been wronged, I can finally exact justice.

Shit. The police have arrived outside. I'm not sure whether Oliver has called them or they traced the call from last night. I should never have let Annie phone them. I wouldn't put it past her to somehow tell them where I was.

Oliver is talking to them now and they've just stopped him from charging back in here.

What am I going to do?

I'm not going back. I'm never going back.

An armed response unit has turned up outside.

Now there are loads of paparazzi.

Shit.

If it's going to end, I'm taking the fucking whore with me. We can both burn in hell.

Annie has started groaning in the kitchen. She says she feels sick. I don't do well with vomit.

Killing her would stop any vomit.

Her phone is ringing again.

I need time to think.

Now they are knocking on the door.

Annie is still groaning.

I'm taking her to the toilet. I swear, if she tries anything, I'll fucking break the bitch's neck.

POLICE EVIDENCE.
CASE AGAINST JESSICA AXE.
DATE OF ARREST: 3RD NOVEMBER 2014.

Just got this book back from the police. It seems it's been almost a year since the last entry.

I own Willow Cottage now and the house next door. It's a very successful business. Since I took it over three months ago, I've had guests stay here almost every week.

It seems this guestbook has proved very popular with the previous guests, so it's probably a good idea to reinstate it.

But I think customer confidentiality was breached by writing the customers' names in the book. If you wish to write something in the book please do, but don't feel you have to include your name unless you want to.

Andrew Drake. 31st October 2015.

✁

181

6th to 9th November
Hetty and William Butterworth

It's good to be back here again. After our wedding in April, we have spent six months travelling around South America, the States, Canada and Alaska. We have seen so much beauty and so much poverty. My favourite places to name but a few were Machu Picchu, the Galapagos Islands, New York, the Rockies and Alaska, all of Alaska, every single part of it, we may have to live there one day. We are staying here for a few days to catch up with friends and family before we move onto Europe and then the Far East.

It's a shame Annie isn't here, it doesn't feel right without her. I do miss her.

⁂

13th to 16th November
Jake, Rosie and Poppy Hamilton

It's been a while since we have been back. We have moved house and changed jobs. It's been a busy year. Most importantly, we have had a beautiful baby girl. After many, many months trying, I finally fell pregnant and Poppy Hamilton was born three months ago. I have never been happier.

Rosie Hamilton

Life is perfect now. I thought it was pretty damned perfect before, but then I held Poppy in my arms and knew that my life was complete. Rosie hasn't stopped grinning since she found out she was pregnant. If at all possible, I think I've fallen even more in love with her.

Jake

That's not entirely true; the sleepless nights were nothing to smile about. Though I wouldn't change them for one single second.

Where is Annie?

We were so looking forward to seeing Annie again and introducing her to our lovely daughter.

Jake

Sunday:
Had a lovely few days playing on the beach with Poppy.

Just been reading back through this book, where the hell is Annie, what happened to her?

❧

20th to 23rd November
Matt, Lucy, Emily and Mia

It's Emily's birthday this weekend and she asked if she could come back here.

I thought it might be weird to bring Lucy here when we have so many memories of being here with Cara. Lucy

has been brilliant though, so supportive. The girls love her. I do too.
  Matt

Wait a minute. You haven't told me you love me yet, but you're quite happy writing it in this book?
  Lucy

I was building up to it.

I was kind of waiting for the right moment.

I love you too.

Awww, isn't that sweet.
  Emily

Shut up, squirt, I know you're rolling your eyes in embarrassment right now. Yes, I love your dad.

It is sweet. Very embarrassing, but very sweet. You've made him smile again. I like that. I'm only going to say this once and if you use it against me, I may have to shave your eyebrows, but I love you too.

Awww, squirt!! That's so nice.

Don't go all sappy on me. I also love Robert Pattinson, Justin Bieber, Olly Murs and all of One Direction.

I love you and Mia very much.

Bleugh!!

WHERE IS DASH?
MIA XXX

That's a good point. Where are Annie and Dash?

Monday:
Had a wonderful weekend with my three favourite girls.

Annie, I don't know if you will read this, no one seems to know where you are. But I'm happy again. I hope you are too.
   Matt

❦

27th to 30th November
The Meechams

We have been twice in the last year and both times we haven't seen Annie, where is she?

The girls love it here, especially when we go out to see the seals. They are getting so big, I wonder how much longer quiet beach holidays and trips to see the seals will keep them amused. We were going to go out to Disneyland this year, but the girls wanted to come back here.

Ha, looking back at our last comments, it's hard to believe me and Ben argued over Barney. We so very rarely argue, so it seems silly that our first proper row was over that.

Barney got married a few months ago to a rather lovely girl called Sally Jenkins. We all came here for the wedding. I would have thought we would have seen Annie then, but she wasn't there. I didn't like to ask where she was, but now I'm getting worried, especially with the last messages in this book.

Rebecca

Where is Annie Butterworth and Mr Butterworth? I've been practising my writing all year and my teacher says it's very good.

Max is no longer a puppy, he got so huge and Mommy was worried he might turn into a horse. He still loves playing on the beach though.

Megan

The seals was grate
Isabelle

❦

For all those asking where Annie Butterworth is, I don't know. I know very little about the previous owner, I suppose I should have asked. I thought she was an old lady who had died. I will ask around to see if any of the villagers know.

Andrew Drake

❦

4th to 7th December
Olly and Annie ~~Butterworth~~ Black

I'm here, I'm safe. I think explanations are in order, some of my old regular guests might be wondering what the outcome of Jessica Axe's little visit was or might be wondering where I am and what I'm doing. Let me tell you.

Let me take you back to the weekend of Jessica Axe.

In fact, I need to go back to the weekend of Judy Fisher, when I fell down a ditch looking for Dash and couldn't get back out. When the whole village came out looking for me. When Olly and I finally got together, I'm not sure what it was that finally brought him to his senses. Nick's will probably had something to do with it. Nick's pet name for me was 'My Happiness', he called me that all the time. So when Judy was confused by Nick leaving Olly a feeling of happiness, it was clear to me and to Olly that Nick was actually giving me to Olly in his will. Or maybe it wasn't that that brought me and Olly together, maybe it was just the right time or maybe it's because I'm a sexual Tyrannosaurus Rex.

I actually spat out my tea reading that.

I don't think it was a case of 'why did I finally want to be with Annie', it was more a case of 'why I wasn't with her before, why did I fight it for so long?'. It wasn't that I was worried what people thought. The only person I was worried about was Nick and if he could see us, what he would think. And I suppose it seemed twisted somehow that he had died and I should benefit from it. But in that time when I thought Annie was dead, that was the lowest point of my life. I know I shouldn't say that when my brother had died, and I loved Nick

187

so much, but Annie... God, the thought of losing her... That was heart-breaking. A life without her was not a life I wanted to live. And then it finally struck me. That's what I was doing by refusing to be with her. What kind of life was I living, denying the thing I wanted most when it was mine for the taking? The will, ha, Nick's foolish sentimental will, was the cherry on the cake, but not the reason. It was nice to know I had his blessing, but I would have been with her anyway, regardless of that. I love her, always have.

And because I'm a sexual Tyrannosaurus Rex.

Yes, that too!

Yes, what Judy Fisher wrote all those months ago was true, every single word. Well, apart from Olly hitting me. I can only presume the groans, thuds, screams and the glass breaking that she heard was us having sex. Again. Yes we did row that morning, but not about being together, that was a done deal. Olly wanted to end it publicly with Vivienne and I wouldn't let him. I didn't want her to look like an idiot in front of the world's press or for her and Darcy's relationship to become widely known until Vivienne was ready. So we agreed to continue our relationship in secret until the time was right for Olly to 'dump' Vivienne. Every week he would come to stay in Willow Cottage on the pretext of writing his autobiography. In reality, we would spend the week in bed together, talking, laughing, making plans and making love. No one knew, though looking back at the messages we left in this book during that time, we weren't exactly subtle.

Then came the weekend of Jessica Axe. A last-minute booking, she phoned and arrived an hour later. Finding out her husband was having an affair was bad enough, but being played by her husband and his best friend was even worse. Knowing that Ryan slept with her purely to help his mate out was hugely depressing and humiliating and it pushed her over the edge. She attacked Anthony. She didn't kill him like she thought she had. She had knocked him unconscious and ... well, not to go into too much detail, but I doubt he'll be having sex ever again, not since she chopped off his most important part.

I knew something was wrong when I phoned the police. They told me that she could be very dangerous. They told me she had attacked her husband, but they didn't go into specifics. They kept asking where she was, but of course I didn't tell them, how could I with Jessica sitting next to me, glaring at me? I just thought she was very scared and perhaps he had attacked her. When she made me stay in the house so I wouldn't phone the police back and tell them where she was, well, that was a little scary, but I didn't think for one minute it was going to turn into a full-blown hostage situation.

Olly turning up and texting me messages about what he wanted to do to me only made things worse. Publicly, he was still very attached to Vivienne so Jessica saw Vivienne as the poor, scorned fiancé and me as the cheating whore. The police turned up, the paparazzi turned up, though quite how they found out I'll never know.

I could see she was getting scared and the looks she was giving me was of pure hatred. I told her I felt sick and eventually she untied me to take me to the toilet. I fought her, grabbed a frying pan and smacked her over the head with it. She hit the floor like a sack of potatoes and I ran outside, straight into the arms of Olly.

Of course he kissed me, passionately, not caring who saw.

189

Unfortunately, the world's press was there and captured it on film for everyone to see. The newspapers were filled with it the next day. And the world waited to see what Vivienne's reaction would be. Olly and Vivienne had planned a big 'break-up' for the following week and so it seemed we had accidentally brought that 'break-up' forward. We expected her to stick to the script and fall into the loving, caring arms of her best friend Darcy and then for her to come out officially a few months later. Although Olly was never supposed to come out of his 'relationship' with Vivienne as the bad guy, we had all gotten what we wanted out of it. Me and Olly could now be together publicly and Vivienne could now be with Darcy. The press hounded us for days and poor Olly got a right bashing in the papers.

Then Vivienne gave an exclusive interview, promising to give her full reaction to Olly's betrayal. Instead, as the interview went out live, Vivienne confessed to everything, that the whole relationship was a sham, that she had persuaded Olly to be her 'fiancé', that she had been too scared to come out and declare her love for Darcy to the British press, but now she wasn't going to hide it any longer. She actually made Olly out to be quite the hero and that he had been forced to keep his relationship with me quiet for months. The press followed us around for a few days and left us alone after that.

Until we got married. They were very interested in that.

And what of Jessica Axe? Well, she was arrested for her assault on her husband and kidnapping me but, thankfully, it was clear the woman was very unhinged and she is now getting some much-needed counselling and therapy. Many of her friends and family vouched for her that she was normally a very sane, very together kind of person. The court case is due for next year. I am not pressing charges for her kidnap and assault on me. I'm sure we've all had moments when you want to wrap your hands round someone's throat and shake the life out of them. I remember one such moment when my now husband phoned me in Wales to tell me my cottage had burned down. Finding out he had lied to me after a seven-hour drive back from Wales resulted in many such 'how do I kill him' fantasies. Many of us have the good sense not to act on these fantasies; Jessica Axe lost her good sense that weekend and I hope the judge recognises that and doesn't punish her for a moment of madness.

You're too soft. I personally would like her thrown in jail for the rest of her life.

Olly!

The woman nearly killed my wife, I'm not going to forgive that so easily.

So yes, now I'm married and I couldn't be happier. Our first anniversary will be New Year's Day.

And, like Hetty, we have done a bit of travelling too. We actually met up with her and William in Chicago and they stayed with us for a while in New York. But getting pregnant put a temporary stop to our travels and we came back to Olly's flat in London instead.

So now I'm fat. I swear if I give birth to a baby cow next week, I won't be at all surprised.

I bloody well will be. The scan showed no signs of udders or horns.

And you're not fat, you're the most beautiful woman in the world. Always have been, always will be.

Still not sexy enough to be in one of your books though, eh?

What, Fat Annie Butterworth, not a chance.

Ow!

You know I love you, now there's more of you to love.

The baby was supposed to be here by now; we booked this weekend thinking that we could bring our child to meet all our family and friends. If the baby does not arrive this weekend, I'm being induced on Tuesday.

I wouldn't actually mind if I had the baby here, it seems fitting somehow.

We are not having our baby in this cottage, we are having him in hospital where there are doctors and medicines and machines to help if anything goes wrong.

Nothing will go wrong. And who says the baby will be a he?

We have tried everything to bring on the labour. I've had spicy curries, long walks, hot baths and we even had sex, which was the funniest experience I've ever had, we couldn't stop laughing throughout. But to no avail. The baby seems quite content to stay in there, where it's warm.

I'm going to bed now, need to conserve my energy for when we have sex again tomorrow.

Really?

Oh yes, I'm actually feeling very horny.

Oh, OK then, if I must.

Like it's a hardship for you. You were the one that suggested sex might be the answer.

Purely to get the baby to come, it was completely altruistic.

Yeah right. Come upstairs and rub my back, it's starting to ache again. Maybe this is it!!!!

We are not having our baby here.

Saturday:
Shit, shit, shit!

**Turn the page for an exclusive extract from
Holly Martin's *A Home on Bramble Hill*...**

A feel-good, romantic
comedy to make you smile

A Home on Bramble Hill

HOLLY MARTIN

Prologue

Joy crouched down behind the bush, her heart hammering against her chest. Someone had called the police and now, after two years, she was finally going to get caught.

Her car was hidden in the dark trees behind her and she glanced towards it, trying to decide whether to make a run for it. It was quite far, maybe a hundred metres or more. She peered through the leaves at her would-be captor. He was a lot older than she was and held a bit of weight on his stomach. She was certain she could outrun him. But running would draw his attention, as would the noise of the engine.

She couldn't get caught, her life would be over.

The policeman walked slowly towards where she was and she tried to make herself as small as possible. He was only a few metres away now. If she was going to run, now was the time to do it.

Suddenly, another policeman came round the edge of the house with a dog; a great, snarling Alsatian.

'Come on Phil, there's nothing there,' the dog handler called. 'There's no sign of a break in, no damage, it was probably just kids messing about. They'll be long gone by now. Or shall I release Tiger; he's dying for a run around?'

Tiger? Joy swallowed as she felt cold sweat prickle her neck.

'Keep that savage beast on the lead, you know we don't see eye to eye,' Phil called back, rubbing his bum as he obviously remembered his last run in with the evil hound.

Tiger and his owner disappeared back round the house and with a last look in her direction Phil turned away too.

Just then her stomach gurgled loudly and Phil whipped back to face her, grabbing his baton like it was a loaded gun.

'Colin!' called Phil.

Her heart in her mouth, she leapt up and ran.

'Oi! Police!' yelled Phil. 'Stay where you are.'

Joy leapt over a log and tore through the trees. Behind her she heard Tiger bark and she pushed herself faster. The branches caught her clothes and hair, like fingers dragging her back.

Black metal gleamed in the moonlight and she ran for it. She threw her rucksack into the passenger seat as torchlight danced through the trees towards her.

She quickly started the car, threw it into reverse and seconds later she hit the road. Thanking her brother for teaching her the darker side of how to drive, she slammed her foot on the brake and spun the wheel, executing a perfect J-turn manoeuvre, before tearing off up the road.

The road stayed empty behind her.

She took the first turn off and her wheels screeched as she took several other corners in quick succession. She turned the engine off as she parked outside a quiet, unassuming row of cottages and threw herself across the passenger seat.

A minute later she heard the sound of the police car tearing along the main road. The siren faded into the distance and she knew she was safe.

With a shaky hand, she pushed her hair from her face and waited for her heart to stop pounding. That was close, too close.

Chapter One

'Please let me lick it,' Joy said.

'Uh uh, no way, not in my car,' Alex said. 'I'm driving as fast as I can. Bloody stupid country lanes, could you have picked anywhere more remote than this to live?'

She smiled as they passed the village sign: 'Bramble Hill; Voted Britain's Friendliest Village for the Last Nine Years.'

'I love that it's in the middle of nowhere. It's so cute and quiet. Fifty-six people live in this village Al, can you imagine. Pretty soon I'll know them all by name. There'll be Mrs Twinkly Eyes who will invite me in for a slice of homemade lemon drizzle cake whilst she regales me with stories from her youth. Mr Silver Hair who will come round to offer advice on my garden, and lovely mummies who will invite me round for coffee and we'll chat in the garden whilst the angelic little cherubs play quietly nearby. And there's a local pub, a proper local. Do you know how long I've wanted a proper local? Somewhere the landlord knows your name, knows your usual tipple and has it waiting for you on the bar as soon as you walk in. There'll be cake sales and village fairs and people will give me eggs and fresh vegetables in return for my delicious apple pies. I can't wait.'

She surreptitiously licked a tiny droplet of chocolate ice cream off her hand and looked up at Alex who was smiling at her.

'What?'

'What's it like in your head Joy, is everything slightly rose-tinted? Your glass is permanently overflowing isn't, it? When it rains you smile because it's good for the garden. Joy by name, Joy by nature.'

She smiled at the turn of phrase he had used for years as he pulled up outside the house.

He leaned over her looking out on the tiny whitewashed cottage. 'Are you sure about this place? It's quite close to Blueberry Farm.'

She frowned slightly. 'I know. That wasn't my intention. When I agreed to move here, I had no idea it was so close. Maybe it's fate though; maybe it's time I came home.'

His face darkened at this. It was the same disagreement they'd had for the last few years. He put his fingers to his heart. 'Home is in here, you know that, it's not a much-revered bunch of bricks. And you shouldn't allow fate, tradition or sentiment to dictate where you live. You just need to open your heart to new possi-bilities.' He brushed a stray hair from her face. 'This is a fresh start for you; I hope you get everything you want from this.'

'I've had a lot of fresh starts and none of them worked. But I have a good feeling about this place.' She ignored the protest that Alex was quickly forming and pressed on. 'It's not just its proximity to Blueberry Farm. There's something about here that feels like coming home.' She negotiated the door handle with her little finger and carefully clambered out, holding the two ice creams precariously in her hands. 'You'll see. Moving here will be the best thing that has ever happened to me.'

She ignored the look from Alex. Admittedly, she'd said that for the previous eight places she had lived in over the last few years, but this time she hoped it would be different. She turned back towards the house and walked straight into someone.

'Oh sorry.' Joy leapt back and to her horror realised that the man now had two large round chocolate stains on his gleaming, white shirt – almost as if two fake breasts had been painted on. An expensive shirt too, she recognised the little logo on the breast pocket.

'Oh god, I'm so sorry, I...'

He glared down at her and then down at his shirt in shock. She balanced the ice creams in one hand and fished a tissue from her pocket. But as she started to wipe away the ice cream, all she succeeded in doing was mushing the chocolate stain into a larger area across his shirt. He stood watching her as she desperately tried to get some off but made the stain bigger every time she touched him. Now tissue bits were sticking themselves to the shirt too. She abandoned the tissue, which was now hanging off him, and used her hand instead. As she felt his heart thud against her fingers, he abruptly caught her hand and moved it off him.

Joy's mouth went dry. The man was huge, the largest man she had ever seen in her life. He was almost like a bear in terms of size and build, the hand that had pushed her own hand away was like a giant paw. His hair was a shaggy, dirty blond mess that fell across his eyes. Slate grey eyes, like thunderclouds.

In stark contrast to the angry bear before her, a shaggy grey mongrel stood at his side, wagging his tail, his tongue falling out of his mouth in what looked like an amused grin.

Emboldened by the dog's smile, she tried one of her own. 'I really am very sorry. I'll pay to have your shirt cleaned of course and...'

Suddenly, Alex was by her side, obviously sensing there was trouble brewing.

'Hey, there's no harm done here – we'll pay to have your shirt cleaned or for a new shirt, and as it was obviously an accident it would be a shame to start off on the wrong foot. This is Joy, your new neighbour, and I'm Alex, her brother.'

Joy watched as the big man tore his glare away from her and his eyes slid to Alex.

'Brother?' he asked, deliberately ignoring Alex's outstretched hand.

Alex nodded.

'For Christ's sake,' he muttered as he stormed away.

'Well, you certainly know how to make a good first impression,' Alex said.

'I'm sure I can win him round.'

'I'm sure you can. You're my favourite person in the world and if he can't see how fantastic you are, then he's blind.'

Joy passed Alex his rather squished ice cream and followed him into the house. She glanced back at the large man disappearing down the road and tried to ignore the butterflies that were fluttering with unease around her stomach.

The sun was setting over Bramble Hill as Joy drove down towards the tiny village with the last load of her stuff. She had picked it up from Alex's house, nearly an hour's drive from her new home, and waved away offers for him to spend the first night with her.

Next to the village sign she'd just passed was another that she hadn't noticed before. It was weather-beaten, decorated in tiny delicate flowers and said; "Bramble Hill, Home of Finn Mackenzie." She wondered who that might be; the village founder perhaps, or some old scout leader who had taken boys camping and taught them how to make fires since before she was born. She was sure she would find out over the next few days.

The village looked beautiful basked in the rosy glow of the sun as she drove down the hill towards the cluster of whitewashed cottages. It was peaceful and quiet. There was a tiny duck pond, glinting pink and gold as the little white ducks bobbed on the water, an old beamed pub, called charmingly The Peacock's Pride, a tiny shop, and that was it. Life here would be as idyllic and quiet as the village itself.

She drew up outside her house and sighed. Home, sweet home.

Opening her boot, she hefted her large chainsaw over her shoulder, picked up a smaller one and grabbed a bag of some of her other power tools.

'Hey, would you like some help?' came a voice from behind her.

She turned to see a man hurrying towards her. It was the smile she saw first – an honest, genuine smile that spread to his denim blue eyes. He was quite broad in the shoulder, and wearing very tight jeans. His dark hair was floppy over his eyes, in a sexy, unruly, unkempt kind of way.

Although she had carried the large chainsaw many times over the years and she was used to the weight, she wasn't about to turn down an offer of help from someone – it might appear rude. Besides, he was the first person who had actually spoken to her since she had arrived.

'Sure, that would be great.' She carefully passed the chainsaw into his waiting hands.

'This isn't the twelve tonnes of makeup and hair products I was expecting,' he said, following her into the house.

She smiled at the dig. 'I've already unpacked that.'

'Now if my detective skills haven't let me down, you must be Jo Carter.'

'I'm afraid they have. Joy Cartier, my landlord is Joe Carter.'

He was clearly thrown by this.

'I know, weird isn't it? Similar sounding names, but no relation.'

'This could be a problem,' he mumbled, clearly more to himself than to her. She looked at him waiting for clarification but his lovely smile quickly returned and he changed the subject. 'I'm Casey Fallowfield, my brother Zach lives next door. This place looks great.'

They walked through the house and towards the shed. 'Thanks, though I can't take any of the credit. Joe did all the decorating. I'm just renting from him. Just put that on the shelf up there.'

The shed was very small and Casey leaned up over her to put the chainsaw on the shelf, revealing a flash of brown, toned belly. She swallowed. He was standing so close and his fresh citrus smell made something clench in her stomach.

He flashed her a grin as he let go of the chainsaw and she blushed. He knew she had just been staring at his stomach.

'So the chainsaws, what are they for?'

'Cutting wood,' she said.

'This is a very expensive chainsaw though, and are those your initials engraved onto the side?'

She brushed past him as she headed out the shed.

'You're not… The Dark Shadow are you?' He grinned, clearly not believing she was.

She laughed. 'Isn't he supposed to be some eight-foot-tall alien, or a time traveller, or a demon from the underworld?' Some of the conspiracy theories surrounding The Dark Shadow were ridiculous.

'I heard it was animals, trying to send us a message. Or fairies, definitely fairies.'

'I heard—' she looked around to make sure no one was listening '—that it was a Scotsman.'

Casey gasped theatrically. 'Nooooo.'

'A nine-foot Scotsman with a twelve-foot-long red beard, eyes of coal, arms of steel, teeth made from razor blades.'

'Those Scotsmen are savage.'

'Well I'm sure the Scottish are perfectly wonderful people, it's just this one that's savage. Some say he's actually a vampire and he's hundreds of years old. Can I offer you a beer?'

'Sure, then you can tell me about the chainsaws.'

She smiled at him over her shoulder. 'You're nosy, aren't you?'

'People interest me – you interest me, Joy. Where have you come from? Why did you come here? Was it to run away from something or towards something? What do you do for a job? Though it must be something good to afford the rent in this place… and what's with the hulking great autographed chainsaw in your shed?'

'Wow, those are a lot of questions.' She passed him a beer and came back to stand on the decking, watching the sun sink behind the hills. 'Maybe one day I'll tell you the answers.'

'Ah, a woman of mystery. I suddenly like you a whole heap more.'

She chinked her beer against his. 'To friendship then, and to sucking out all the gory details of each other's personal lives.'

'I like it, that's what true friendship is all about; being beholden to each other over our deepest darkest secrets.'

She smiled. 'So what are yours?'

'I'll need more than just a sip of beer inside me to tell you that.'

She turned back to the view.

Just then, the large man she had literally bumped into earlier walked out into his garden. Her heart leapt. He wasn't wearing a top and his whole body seemed to shout muscles. He was so tall, nearly two feet taller than her tiny five feet. He was filthy and sweaty and Joy had never been so turned on in her entire life.

She watched him pick up a large tree, as easily as if he was picking up a daffodil, and place it carefully into a large hole. He patted the soil gently around it, as if the tree was made from china. More soil was added until the tree was secure. He stood up and drank long and deep from a bottle of water. As he moved, the sunlight caught a piercing in his nipple. Joy tried to swallow but realised her throat was now parched. She took a long swig of beer before she remembered Casey standing next to her.

She quickly turned to him, blushing furiously at the thought that he would have caught her gawping so avidly. To her surprise his attention was well and truly caught by the beautiful man next door as well. His eyes, as she imagined hers were right now, were dark with lust and desire.

Joy took another sip of beer, whilst she pondered this, watching the man next door pick up his tools and take them to his shed. As he turned back, he caught them watching, scowled first at her and then broke into a huge grin when he saw Casey and waved at him before going back into his own house.

Casey took a long sip of beer, which he had clearly forgotten about whilst he had enjoyed the show, and then looked at Joy in what he clearly hoped was a nonchalant way.

She arched an eyebrow at him and he sighed.

'That… was Finn Mackenzie, my best friend and the man I've been secretly in love with for the last fifteen years.'

Joy smiled at him in sympathy. Unrequited love was the worst.

He chinked his beer against the side of hers, dryly. 'Come inside and we can start on at least one of my dark and gruesome secrets.'

She followed him in, and sensing this unburdening was going to need a bit more than cheap beer, she grabbed a bottle of wine from the fridge and a huge slab of chocolate. She went through to the lounge where Casey was already sitting on the sofa with his head in his hands.

'You saw it didn't you, the way I looked at him,' he said.

'What, the same look of desire that I had on my face? Yes, I saw it.'

Casey looked up with a sheepish smile. 'He is beautiful, isn't he?'

Joy shook her head with admiration and sat down next to him. 'He's magnificent. If we're sharing secrets, I might as well share mine with you. When I saw that pierced nipple, I wanted nothing more than to run over and lick it.'

Casey laughed, loudly. 'Oh, I know. I went with him when he got that done. It gave me a good excuse to touch it, you know, purely out of curiosity.'

She grinned. 'Of course.'

Darcy, her great, beloved Newfoundland, hauled herself up

from the cool tiled fireplace to finally greet the new visitor. Casey stroked her absently, but his smile faltered as he thought. 'Do you think he saw how I was looking at him?'

'I doubt it. Men are blind to these things. Besides, he waved at you. All I got was a scowl.'

'Yeah, I clocked that. It's your hair, he has a thing about redheads, can't stand them.'

Joy felt her mouth pop open. 'That's a bit… hairist.'

Casey smiled again. 'To be fair, he's anti-all-women at the moment.'

'Oh… so he's gay as well?'

Casey laughed even louder at this. 'Oh god, I wish. That would be all my Christmases, birthdays, dreams and wishes come true in one fell swoop. No, Finn is straight. He just hates women after his ex-wife cheated on him. He hasn't been with anyone since. Though not from lack of offers from the entire female population of Bramble Hill and the other local villages. They were queuing up once Pippa left, but he hasn't shown a flicker of interest. He has been sullen to the point of rude and still they fancy their chances.'

'Maybe his marriage broke up because he was gay.'

'You're just saying that to cheer me up. No, he's definitely straight. But it's not just women he has a problem with. He's rude to everyone; well, he has been for the last eighteen months. So don't take it personally. He says very little, keeps himself to himself, never gets involved with village life. Never gets involved with anyone. You'll be no different. Well, except that you have red hair. He'll hate you for that.'

Joy frowned.

'Pippa was a redhead so now he has tarred all redheads with the same brush,' Casey explained as he finished his beer and opened the wine.

'And how do the villagers take to his rudeness?'

'They love him.' Casey obviously saw the look of confusion on her face. 'You know who he is, right?'

She shook her head.

'Finn Mackenzie, the actor?'

She shrugged, still none the wiser.

'He was in that vampire trilogy years ago – *In the Darkness, The Taste of Blood* and, my personal favourite, *The Spoils of War*. God, that bit when he bathes naked in the moonlit lake… I think I ruined my video by pausing it so often in the same place. I should have realised back then that I was gay, when all my friends were drooling over the beautiful Scarlet Rome and all I could see was Finn.'

He must have seen the blank look on her face.

'You haven't seen them, really? You must be the only living woman not to. What exactly were you doing twenty years ago?'

'I was nine, so…' She trailed off as she realised exactly what she was doing twenty years before.

'You might have been a bit young to appreciate the first film, but the second and the third? How could it have passed you by?'

She shrugged. 'I guess it did.'

'He was fourteen when he filmed the first one and nineteen by the time the last one came out. Overnight he became this Hollywood sensation, the press followed him around everywhere. He hated it. I don't think he had any idea what it would be like for him to be famous overnight. After *Spoils* was finished he withdrew from public life. He had so many offers to do so many different projects, but he wasn't interested at all. He hasn't done anything for the last fifteen years.'

She smiled at Casey's enthusiasm for Finn. 'I guess it's safe to say, you're his biggest fan.'

'I am, yes, but we've been friends since we were both knee high to a grasshopper. It wasn't the fame thing that attracted me. Hell, you've seen him – the man's a god.'

'I take it you haven't told him how you feel?'

'Good lord, no, definitely not. No one knows I'm gay. You're the first person I've told, and I wouldn't have told you if you hadn't caught me drooling. I'm normally better at disguising it than that. Well, I hope I am.'

Joy frowned slightly. 'You've been gay for fifteen years and never told anyone?'

'No. Not really. I mean yes, my inappropriate crush on my best friend has lasted fifteen years but I guess I never really accepted I was gay until recently. A year, maybe two.'

'But why haven't you told your parents? Would they be awful about it?'

Casey poured two large glasses of wine, broke off a huge chunk of chocolate and shoved it in his mouth. It took him a few moments to answer whilst he chewed on it.

'Honestly, I think they would have been OK with it. I come from a very loving family and all they've ever wanted was for me and Zach to be happy. But I think their friends would give them hell over it. They're... Mum's incredibly wealthy and there's always social gatherings – balls, seven-course dinners, big charity events that they used to attend with Lord and Lady Chalsworth, the Earl of Menton Hall, and Sir Ronald Chase-Matthews.' He affected a posh voice as he reeled off his fellow socialites. 'I've always shied away from it myself, which I think disappointed them slightly. Zach is more into the social networking, keeping up with the Joneses malarkey than I am. As the oldest son, they would have loved nothing more than if I attended these functions with some beautiful lady on my arm. If I were to turn up with a beautiful man on my arm instead... well, I don't think their friends would be as understanding.'

Joy broke off a chunk of chocolate and chewed on it, thought-fully. 'So you're never going to tell them?'

'I suppose, if I found someone I loved, truly loved and who loved me too, then perhaps I would be brave enough to say, "this is the man that I'm going to spend the rest of my life with". But it's hard to find that man when no one knows I'm actually gay.'

'My brother's gay,' Joy said and then laughed at the look on his face. 'No, don't worry. I wasn't trying to set you up with him. I hate that when people do that to me, "oh you're single, he's single, why don't the two of you get together?" No, you're not his type at all. Alex prefers big men, just as you do it seems. No, I just meant maybe he could take you out to some gay bars, give you a chance to meet some men that are in the same boat.'

'He's… openly gay?'

She nodded.

'And how did your parents take to that?'

'They didn't. They were both killed in a car accident when he was seventeen. I'm not sure if he had even figured it out by that point. He came out to me a few years later.'

'Oh god Joy, I'm so sorry, that's terrible. Your parents being killed obviously, not your brother being gay.'

She swallowed the lump in her throat that was always there when she spoke about her parents. 'It's fine. It's been twenty years.'

'You were nine?'

She nodded again.

'That's what you were doing twenty years ago. I was fawning over my best friend dressed in leather and you were mourning the loss of your parents. I'm sorry. Who raised you after they'd died?'

'Al did. He was three weeks away from being eighteen. He lied about his age, told the authorities he was eighteen and as such was my legal guardian. By the time they checked, he was eighteen.'

'He raised you on his own?'

She smiled. 'I know, looking back, I just took it for granted that he was there. He had always been there, always would be there for me. I didn't think until I was eighteen myself what he should have been doing – that going clubbing, getting drunk, going to parties should have been a way of life for him. He wanted to go to university, train to be in the film industry. He

210

put it all on hold to look after me. He did a superb job too. He wasn't just my brother, he was my dad, my mum and my friend. Can you imagine, when all his friends were graduating university, or coming back from travelling the world, he was sitting down with me explaining to me about periods. He was amazing.'

'Sounds like someone I'd like to meet.'

'You should, just so you have at least one gay friend to talk to about all this stuff. Maybe he can help you to come out to your family. Or at least help you find someone other than Finn to set your sights on.'

Just then there was a loud knock on the door.

Casey stretched back into the sofa. 'Well, I don't think we've done too badly in the sharing of our deepest, darkest secrets for one night. Maybe we'll stop there before I discover that the chainsaw is for hacking up bodies.'

'Damn it, now I'm going to have to kill you too.' She moved to answer the door and Darcy followed.

Joy opened it and the man standing on the doorstep was so obviously Casey's brother, Zach. He had the same washed denim eyes, the same black floppy hair, but where Casey's unkempt style had probably taken seconds to achieve, Zach's unruly 'I don't care about my hair' look had probably taken hours of styling. He had the sexy designer stubble in comparison to Casey's clean-shaven face. But feeling horribly disloyal to her new friend, she had to admit that Zach had the edge when it came to sex appeal.

'What have you done with my brother?' asked Zach, his mouth twitching into a smirk. 'I know he's in there with you. I saw him carry that chainsaw into your house, and he hasn't come out since. If you've chopped him up into tiny pieces you'll have me to answer to.'

She fixed him with a dark look. 'Why don't you come down to the cellar and I'll show you what I've done with him.'

'Ha, I've seen that film. I go down to the cellar with you and

211

the next thing I'm manacled to a table as you cut out my innards. Not a chance. Unless it's bondage you're into, then I wouldn't mind a bit of manacling.'

She laughed. 'I'm Joy, you must be Zach?'

'Ah, he mentioned me, did he – just before you brutally murdered him?'

Just then Casey appeared behind her. 'Fret not little brother, she tried to kill me, but I fought her off. Are you ready to go down the pub?'

'Yep, is the murderer coming with us?'

'She sure is. We'll introduce her to the *friendly* folk down The Pride.'

Joy couldn't fail to miss the sarcastic way Casey had said friendly.

'Hey, they're OK… just not keen on newcomers,' Zach said. 'They'll take a while to warm to you but I'm sure you'll win them round.' He moved closer to her, his eyes casting over her. She stroked Darcy, a useful prop to focus on as she found herself embarrassed by the sheer hunger in his eyes.

Casey moved to stand by her side, forcing Zach to move back a bit. 'Go and grab my wallet would you, I left it on the coffee table.'

Zach nodded and with a last dark look in her direction, he scooted back to his house. Joy tried to calm her heart down before she turned back to Casey. What was wrong with her? Three times her pulse had quickened in the last half hour, each time with someone different. It had clearly been too long since she'd been with a man.

Casey closed the door behind Zach and turned to her.

'I like you Joy, so let me give you one piece of advice. Don't get involved with my brother. Women are like a game to him. He'll lavish you with attention and charm but once he's had you, he'll move onto the next. If he had notches on his bedpost, he would've gone through several bedposts by now. I shudder to think how many women he's actually slept with. Don't be one of them. Now—' he opened the door and offered her his arm '—let me escort you down The Pride.'

Zach was already waiting with his dark looks of appreciation. Joy sighed inwardly; she really didn't need to get involved with a serial womaniser. And with her definitely not being Casey's type, and Finn hating the ground she walked on, it didn't seem her dry patch would be ending any time soon.

Dear Reader,

Thank you so much for taking the time to read this book – we hope you enjoyed it! If you did, we'd be so appreciative if you left a review.

Here at HQ Digital we are dedicated to publishing fiction that will keep you turning the pages into the early hours. We publish a variety of genres, from heartwarming romance, to thrilling crime and sweeping historical fiction.

To find out more about our books, enter competitions and discover exclusive content, please join our community of readers by following us at:

🐦 @HQDigitalUK

f facebook.com/HQDigitalUK

Are you a budding writer? We're also looking for authors to join the HQ Digital family! Please submit your manuscript to:

HQDigital@harpercollins.co.uk.

Hope to hear from you soon!

DIGITAL HQ

If you enjoyed *The Guestbook at Willow Cottage*, then why not try another delightfully uplifting romance from HQ Digital?